S. A. Gordon

Midwest Book Review about S.A. Gorden's previous novels:

"... *The Deuce of Pentacles* is a harrowing yet thrilling saga which is recommended to mystery buffs and readers with an interest in the paranormal. Also highly recommended are Gorden's two previous novels: *Faces of Doom* ... and the "double novel", *Days Between Seasons/Crystal Clear Pond...*"

The Pioneer -- Bemidji Minnesota

... S.A. Gorden has produced four suspense novels ... (They) feature gripping storylines well larded with action, sex and violence ... stories that have an edge to them.

Taconite Runes books by S.A. Gorden

The Deuce of Pentacles
Faces of Doom
Days Between Seasons and Crystal Clear Pond

Eyes of an Eagle

by S.A. Gorden

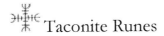 Taconite Runes

This book is a work of fiction. Characters, names and incidents are based on the author's imagination. Any resemblance to actual events or persons is coincidental.

Taconite Runes
42302 Chase Lake Road
Deer River, MN 56636

ISBN: 0-9719471-3-9
Library of Congress Control Number: 2002114552

Cover design Taconite Runes

Preface
From a legend of the Oceti Shakowin of the Lakota

A young man skilled in hunting one day left the village in search of meat. He spotted an elk. He had a new bow with a quiver full of straight arrows, yet the elk managed to stay just out of range. Deep in the woods, the tracks and elk disappeared.

Night came to the thick forest and there was no moon. The young man realized he was lost. He came upon a cool, clear stream. Refreshed from the water, he ate his pack food. Curling up in his fur robe he tried to sleep, but the forest was full of strange sounds. The cries of the night animals, the hooting of the owls, the rustling of the trees all sounded new and different.

Suddenly, there was a new sound. It was something neither he nor any other living creature had heard before. Afraid, the man pulled the robe close about him. Clutching his bow in one hand and his knife in another, the young man listened. The mournful sound became a song both beautiful and sad. The song was full of love and yearning.

The young man fell asleep. In his dreams, the redheaded woodpecker came. He sang the beautiful song and said, "Follow me and I will teach the song to you."

When the young man woke, the sun was already high in the sky. In the tree, above him tapped a redheaded woodpecker. When he got to his feet, the bird fluttered to the next tree and waited. The young man followed. The woodpecker flew to another tree and then another. For the rest of the morning, the bird led the man through the forest. Finally, the young man heard the song again. Walking past the last line of trees, he heard the drumming of the woodpecker and saw the bobbing of the red head in a cedar tree. As he got closer, he saw the bird was beating on a branch filled with holes that it had made. A breeze blew through the forest and the woods were filled again with the music.

The young man watched and listened and discovered that the hollow branch was making the beautiful music. He climbed the tree and broke off the branch the wind was singing through. He called the watching woodpecker a friend. He thanked the redheaded bird for the gift he had made.

When the young man got back to his village, he hid in his tipi and tried to make the branch sing. He blew hard on the branch and then soft. He held it in one hand and then the other. He swung it through the air, but no sound came.

The young man then went to the sweat lodge. After, he climbed a lonely hill. For four days and four nights without food or water, he cried for a vision, which would show him how to make the song. With his head resting on a large rock during the last night of his quest, the redheaded woodpecker came to him in the night breeze. The woodpecker turned himself into a man. Cautioning the youth to watch carefully, the redheaded man showed him how to make the branch sing.

Awaking the next day from the vision, the young man found a cedar tree. Breaking off a branch the length of his forearm, he used his bow-drill and knife to whittle the cedar wood branch. The shape he whittled was of a bird with a long neck and open beak. He painted the bird's head sacred red. He smoked the branch with sage, cedar, and sweet grasses. He put his mouth to the flute calling his bride and his destiny in the beautiful melancholy music. And the redheaded bird watched.

From the Kalevala

Vainamoinen was born an old man from the sea, the ageless singer and harpist. His mother was air-daughter and his father the foam raised by the strong east wind. Vainamoinen's song brought the small man from the sea who chopped down the evil old oak. Vainamoinen had a sharp axe made, cleared the land and sowed the seven seeds he found. He left one birch tree standing in the cleared fields. The eagle stopped and rested there. Curious, the eagle asked Vainamoinen why he left the birch in the middle of the fields. "So you will have a place to rest," he replied. The cuckoo stopped and rested on the birch. Curious, he asked Vainamoinen why he left the birch in the middle of the fields. "So you will have a place to rest," he replied. All the creatures of the air stopped and rested on the birch tree. They watched and listened to Vainamoinen sing the eternal magical songs and play his enchanting harp.

When the Day-god rises over the land of Kaleva and the heat of midday comes, the birds still rest in the birch trees. The leaves of the birch still whisper the melody of the harp and the echo of the songs of the man of quiet water, the knower eternal, Vainamoinen. And the birds still watch.

Chapter 1
Watching

I spent the morning being watched by an eagle. This was the day of the week I did outside work. It was early fall. The leaves were just beginning to change. The light frost had melted and the grass had dried enough for me to start mowing the lawn. I had just finished mowing one track around the lawn when he flew in.

He came in low from the slight rise in the west. I saw the dark shape crest the tree line and started immediately to reject the shapes it wasn't. Not a crow ... too big. Not a heron ... wrong neck. Not a hawk ... An eagle! He flew right in front of me and landed in the tallest tree in the yard. As he spread his wings in landing, I saw the white head and a small white spot. He was a young bird then; maybe that was why he landed?

He looked at me mowing. I knew how good the eagle's eyes were. He could have watched me from across the farmer's field to the east. Why did he come here? I cut the grass watching the bird as he watched me. He tracked my movements with his eyes, across and up and down the yard. As I mowed under the tree waiting for him to take flight, the minutes stretched to an hour and still he watched. Every time my back was toward him, I could feel his eyes. When I couldn't stand the prickly sensation on the back of my neck, I would twist around and there he watched with his head canted to one side.

I turned a corner with the mower and looked. He was gone! I scanned the empty sky, the far tree line looking for the familiar shape. Why had he come? Why had he chosen me to watch? The back of my neck tingled; I looked and saw nothing. But I felt the eyes, the eyes of an eagle watching. In my mind I saw the raptor cock his head and fluff his feathers as he watched. What was he thinking when he watched? Did he think me strange for staying on the ground? Or did he envy the way I easily covered the yard? Or was there something else? Somehow I knew there was something else to those watching eyes.

***

The Chameleon was a scout infiltrator. He worked for a group known to themselves as the Users. Referring to the Chameleon, as a he, could be wrong. The only one who still might know the gender of the Chameleon is the Chameleon. Depending on the infiltration, the Chameleon could be a male, female, neutral or somewhere in-between.

The Users would move into a community. After living in the neighborhood for possibly years, they would leave, stripping it of everything they could take. This would be more than just the material wealth of the community. The Users would scavenge the intellectual and social fabric of the society. Local companies would be taken over and sold. Copyrights, plans, the very soul of the community would be copied and destroyed. When the Users were done with a neighborhood, it would be a hollow shell of what it had been. It would take decades, if ever, for the community to recover. By then the Users, richer than before, would have sucked dry the life of other communities. Stronger, they would wait for the chance to return to harvest the strength of the region again.

The Chameleon waited and watched learning all he could about the new objective before becoming a member of the community. The Chameleon was a legend among the Users. He, in his various disguises, had infiltrated dozens of communities planning their rape. The Chameleon was the only scout never to run afoul of the local authorities. The Chameleon's existence was a lonely one. The little pleasure he took was from the theft of the happiness of the individuals living in the community, his goal, the success of his family, the Users.

He watched. Which gender would give him the most access to the community? Which disguise would give him the most pleasure? Which local community was the richest?

***

I am living on the old family farm. Until last year, I lived in Chicago. My father had died five years earlier and just last year my mother had joined him. My brother lives in New York and made it plain to my dad that he never wanted to come back to the farm. Dad had always wanted to keep the farm in the family so when he retired from farming he signed the land over to me with the agreement that I wouldn't move in until both my parents were both gone.

My job is checking technical accuracy of submitted articles and manuscripts for a major textbook/magazine publishing house in Chicago. I like my job. I like Chicago, but I couldn't stand living there. I had worked for the company for twelve years, right out of college. I would only meet my boss twice a year, the Christmas party and the summer Fourth of July picnic. Most of my time, I spent on the computers or at the libraries. I was their fastest proofreader so when I suggested that I would like to work at home they let me. I've been at the farm for eleven months and I'm not sure if my boss yet realizes that 'home' is in a different state.

Before I moved back home, I completely re-wired the old farmhouse. But it still feels like home. All the changes occurred within the walls. My brother's and my old bedrooms are converted into my workroom. I have a small library on the shelves, one top of the line PC, one used PC linked permanently to the Internet, a laptop, and three phone lines. Because of the high cost of living in town, my workroom still costs the company less then my downtown Chicago office space.

The farm itself consists of 160 acres of land, half of which are wooded. The old barn had burned down in an electrical storm ten years ago and had been replaced with a metal equipment shed. My father had changed, during the last few years he had worked the farm, from dairy and beef cattle to planting seed crops and hadn't been forced to replace the barn when it burned. The insurance money from the barn had been a Godsend being that both my father and mother had started to have failing health. The old brick milk house still stood, but most of the equipment inside had either been sold or rusted away. There is a two-stall garage next to the house. One door is the size of an average car while the other is large enough to accommodate a small truck. The house is a small cozy two story salt box with a full basement. The north corner of the basement has our sauna. Firewood is brought down through a chute that opened from the side of the house just above ground level.

As I stepped into the house from the cool fall air, I could smell the warm moist essence of home. With a little bit of trying I could find the smell left from my mother's cooking, the hint of pipe tobacco from before my father quit smoking, the spilled soap from the laundry in the basement, and the mustiness of the household animals.

I entered the workroom. Lying on the warm computer chassis my cat, Move-over, slept. He was a longhaired mottled gray, white, and black animal of about fifteen pounds. When he napped during the day, he would drape himself over the Internet computer. His legs and tail would dangle in the air while his head rested directly above the chassis' fan. For some reason, the cat liked the hum of the fan. I jiggled the computer mouse enough to get the screen to come out of sleep mode. As I waited for the screen to come up with any email messages, the cat raised his hoary scared head and looked at me. Cats always seem to know more than any animal should when they look at you. The aloof stare reminded me of a scientist studying an experiment with me being the subject. After the eagle, the stare bothered me. I scratched the cat's belly knowing he would go to sleep. A rumble came from the animal and his head went down, but when I looked his lids were not closed. The slitted yellow eyes still watched.

In my inbox was an angry message from a scientist, a Nobel-laureate. He had submitted an article for one of my company's magazines. The article was on the dynamics of ecosystems. He had tried to prove that species die-out was caused because ecosystems are inherently unstable and degenerating. I had recommended that the magazine not print the article. It was not up to his previous standards. The scientist had not had anything printed for a while. I felt he had just thrown something together to get his name in print again. I had sent the scientist my review pointing out a series of flaws in his statistical analysis and referencing a number of sources using Chaos math that showed the system would have an inherited complexity not degeneration. I finished with a note that if the concerns about the article were addressed I would recommend it be printed.

It was a good thing for the scientist that the blistering letter was sent email. If it had been sent through the regular mail, it would have been violated a number of laws. I copied it to my cranks file. Someday I will have to go through the file. I'm sure I will soon have enough material to write my own book. I nearly put my computer back into sleep mode, but I noticed that Internet connection was still active and I was having a lot of hard disk accessing. A virus? This was why I had the old computer as my Internet access. All my sensitive files were kept on my other computer. I ran my anti-virus programs and found nothing. I then did a file check with my backup disks. Nothing. I gave up, thinking it was just a quirk in the system.

I was tired by the time I finished my system checks. I went to bed. As I dozed off, I felt the cat climb on top of my chest. I scratched him behind his ears and under his chin. His front paws moved as he kneaded my chest. I had to go to sleep. Tomorrow I would be taking supplies to my uncle. His rumbling purr lulled me to oblivion. Somehow I knew before I drifted off that his eyes were open, watching.

When I woke up, Move-over was gone. I never saw the cat leave. He would just disappear for a few hours or a few days if a local female was in heat. Every so often, he would come back with a new scar or two. He would then stand in front of me and yowl until I would pick him up. A scratch under the chin and a compliment about his fighting prowess, he would jump down and walk away with his tail high in the air for a banner.

Today I didn't think much about the cat. I had to get the canoe on the pickup and my uncle's supplies packed. My uncle was a hermit. He had gone to Vietnam when he was eighteen and served two tours of duty before coming home. When I was younger, I could remember him coming home to the farm every time he lost a job. One day I helped my father and uncle load a canoe with supplies. We drove north to a river that flowed through a number of different state and national forests before entering the Rainy Lake flowage. From the river's edge, we watched my uncle paddle away. We didn't hear from him for two years. He had finally found a place he could live.

He had discovered a pocket of dry land surrounded by northern peat bogs. During the winter months, you could get in by snowshoes. During the other seasons, you could only get in by canoe. He built a shack on the high ground. Every so often, the forestry department would try to force him out. They never tried too hard. To my knowledge, they never saw him except by air. The one time they tried to take apart his shack my uncle stole their canoes. They were taken out of the swamps two days later by helicopter. Their canoes showed up at a landing by Ely a week after that.

Over the years my uncle had a harder and harder time leaving the woods. Dad had started to bring supplies to him three times each year. He would load a canoe and drift down the river. His brother would show up within a matter of hours and they would head for his shack.

I loved my crazy uncle. It was nice having a truly eccentric relative in the family to talk about. He was not a mean or violent man. It was just that no one had helped him come back from Vietnam. When we talked, you could tell there was a part of him not there. He had become a part of his hideaway. Anything that happened around his retreat, he knew about. Without leaving his shack, he knew if one of his snares had been sprung or an animal was in a trap. He seemed to know about the tracks left by the animals traveling though the bogs before he walked up to see them.

Today was a beautiful fall day. I drifted down the river enjoying the clean air and the river sounds. In the years I had spent in Chicago, I could never remember a time without traffic sounds. I never got used to it. I heard the loud deep call of a Pileated Woodpecker followed by the hammering as he searched for food. As I drifted past a bend in the river, I saw a tree on the bank. It had a series of large holes nearly tearing its trunk in half. The base of the tree was covered with large white splinters. The big black and white woodpecker slowly fluttered to the tree. Instead of hammering at the tree or sending a call, the red crested bird turned his head and watched me drift past. The hammering didn't start till I was out of sight.

"That was interesting," said a soft voice from the shore. I jerked so fast I nearly tipped the canoe.

"Ben! I wish you wouldn't sneak up on me." I nosed the canoe into the bank. My uncle pulled his old scarred canoe out from behind some brush and we paddled off in silence. He led me off the river up a small stream. The stream cut its way through a floating bog. Every year the channel through the bog would change, as the floating vegetation would drift to new locations. Finally we came to a section of land that looked like all the rest of the bog, but instead of being just a few inches of dirt and roots floating on water it was a bar of sand and rock. Ben's shack lay just behind a screen of brush a couple of dozen feet from the stream.

My uncle never talked till after the supplies were unloaded and stored away. One of the first things he did was open a can of coffee. He set it brewing in a pot on the old rusty barrel stove he had in the shack. When we finished, he poured me a cup of the scalding hot brew. I had the only cup in the place. Ben poured his own coffee in an old Campbell's soup can. I couldn't help but notice he had a whole rabbit, fur and all, simmering in a pot next to the coffee. I knew I wouldn't be staying for supper.

As we drank, I felt eyes upon me. I started to search the shack. I found the watching eyes. In the corner under an old wood crate, a mouse sat watching me. His little paws groomed his whiskers. His eyes never left my face.

A whisper came from my uncle. "You know, Dan. It was my third time as point man before they started watching me."

"Point Man?"

"When our squad went on patrol, there had to be a man out front. He was the eyes of the squad. If the point man wasn't good, he would get either himself or the squad killed. He had to see the enemy before they saw him. He had to evade the booby traps and mark them for the rest of the squad to avoid.

"The first time I worked the point I nearly got everyone killed in an ambush, but I learned. I liked the point. It was just me and the jungle. It was my third time at point. I was maybe a hundred meters ahead of the rest of the squad. I noticed that the birds had stopped making a ruckus when I walked past. They would watch me pass. Later when the squad followed, they complained but with me they just watched.

"It happened during my second tour... During that patrol, I walked out of the jungle and started across a rice paddy. I felt eyes. The eyes came from my left. I turned and looked back at the edge of the jungle. Finally, I saw the eyes. A VC sniper was watching the paddy. I locked onto his eyes. We must have stared at each other for ten minutes. I could hear the squad coming out of the jungle behind me. The sniper just backed away into the trees.

"The only one of the squad who ever learned about the watching was the sergeant. He was a Nisei from San Francisco. He saw the birds watching me at point halfway through my last tour. He called the birds, Yosei, Japanese fairies. I still remember him whispering, "*Don't tell the rest of the squad.*" A mortar round got the sarge a week later. Blew him in half."

Old Ben took another swallow of coffee. That was the longest he had ever spoken to me at one time. He looked so sad sipping the coffee. The mouse still watched.

Ben got up and rummaged around under the pile of old clothes and tree boughs he called his bed. I always considered it more of a nest than a bed. He came back with a leather sheathed knife. He handed it to me. "This is your Great Grandfather Ilmari's puukko. He brought it with him when he emigrated from Finland. He gave it to me when I was ten. He said that I would need to know how to use a knife. He was right..."

He drank another swallow of coffee. I could see the pain of old memories in his face. With eyes filled with sadness, he said, "It is yours now."

The old leather sheath was scuffed and blackened with age. The varnish on the wood hilt was worn off in places. I pulled the knife from the sheath. In my hand the old knife felt lighter than the knives I had in my kitchen although the blade was nearly twice as thick. The clip blade was a dark rippled gray -- the color high-grade hand-forged carbon steel fades to with age. The edge was honed bright. I turned the blade up. The sharpened edge disappeared. I knew if I just touched the blade with my thumb blood would flow. I turned.

The mouse still watched.

Chapter 2
Waiting

The Chameleon had decided on a community. As far as he could tell, it was the richest and strongest in the whole area. His next decision would be where to infiltrate. The economic heart had a large turnover of individuals. A new face would easily be lost in the crowds. But the economic center also had greater security. The outlying area had less new people moving in but also much less security. Where would be the best place to infiltrate?

Females seemed to have nearly as much access to sensitive materials with less security questions. Males had the most access. Gays were in the minority but would they have the benefit of both the sexes? Which would help the group the most, greater access or less questions?

The Chameleon had time. He waited and watched.

***

When I got home, Move-over was on the computer again. I could feel his eyes on my back as I proofread portions of a college algebra textbook. For some reason, I couldn't concentrate on the reading. I kept remembering back to when I was little. It was summer. I recalled seeing a Disney type Davy Crockett movie or show; I don't remember which. In the show, Davy was in some contest where he threw a knife and an axe at a target. I had an old pocketknife and was trying to throw it at a tree. Dad came up to me.

"Son. You are using the wrong kind of knife for throwing."

He went into the house and came back with an old straight-backed paring knife. We threw the knife for what seemed like hours. He stuck it in the tree every time he threw. At the end, I got it to stick in the tree three times in a row. I vaguely remember keeping up the practice for the rest of the summer but I could only clearly remember that first time with Dad. It was one of the few times we were alone and not arguing.

I got the puukko. In the backyard, the stump of the tree I used for practice so many years ago stood by the foundations of the old burned barn. The first throw -- the knife bounced off the stump. The second stuck. I threw again and again. The blade was starting to sink a half-inch into the wood, three quarters, a full inch.

I suddenly felt eyes. I turned and looked. A crow sat on a fence post his black eye watching. The crow had only one good eye; the other was frosted over. I yelled. He didn't budge but two more crows flew in to join him on the fence line. I notice my arm was sore and I was drenched in sweat. I went inside wondering about Ben, the knife and those watching animals.

As I was making supper, Move-over showed up. For the first time in days, eyes watching me did not give me the willies. Move-over always watched me whenever food was involved. The only movement out of the cat as he watched was the twitching of his tail. It started to snap back and forth when I dished out the food on my plate. As I sat down to eat, the cat gave a mournful yowl. When I didn't acknowledge him, he climbed up on my lap and went to sleep. For some reason, cats feel that they can absorb food directly from someone's stomach if they are lying on it during eating. I don't know. They may be right. With Move-over on my lap, I never feel quite as full after a meal.

The familiarity of the animal's actions had finally

permitted me to forget about being watched. I was able to finish my work for the week with only the continual problem of Net accessing on my Internet computer.

***

Tabitha loved her morning runs. The autumn and spring air was the best. She liked running at home better than when she was at college. The air at school had a tinge of automobile fumes, which clogged her sinuses and at times made her eyes water. This was her fifth year at school trying to get a four-year college degree. Two things were keeping her in school for so long. Her track scholarship was forcing her to keep her spring and fall classes light. Also, the recent budget cuts required that some courses were offered every other year. Even some full-time students had to work five and six years for a standard four-year degree.

This fall none of the courses she needed for her Bachelor of Arts in electrical engineering were being offered. She decided to stay home for the semester and work at her family's business. Most of her track events were in the spring so even without fall classes her scholarship would stay intact. She loved working at the family video store during the summer and semester breaks. It was an easy job. She could watch videos or do her homework with only an occasional disturbance during most of the day. Problems only occurred during the after work or beginning of the weekend rush.

Over the summer and into the fall she had gotten to know most of the regulars. She liked all except for a couple of drunks who would stop in between bars and one mean woman who complained about everything. Sure some of them were troublemakers, like the group of high school boys who would hang out out-front after school or the couple going through a divorce. But basically she considered them okay.

She liked to classify the people that came into the store,

the retired, the teachers, the students, the workers, the homemakers, and the others. This was Thursday. She wondered if the new man was coming into the store. He was too young to be retired. He didn't work regular hours. He drove a clean pickup and was always dressed well so he wasn't a farmer or someone who worked in the woods. He was articulate. He loved to take his time examining the tapes reading the back of the cases carefully. He didn't match up with her classifications, which made her all the more curious.

Tabitha did her after run stretch and showered. She picked up her backpack filled with schoolbooks and supplies and walked the six blocks to the video store. Her brother had opened the store earlier and had a music video blaring from the screen over the counter. Tabitha turned the volume down on her hearing aids and took over the front counter. She got a paperback to read while her brother finished re-stocking the overnight returns. He would leave when he finished and she would then replace the music video with the Alfred Hitchcock movie she started yesterday.

***

Maybe it was the staring, maybe it was the extra hours I took to finish the algebra textbook, but for the first time in months I thought about Hanna. We had been living together for five years and dating the previous two. I broke it off with her just a few months before I left Chicago for home. Hanna was a lovely girl, friendly, astute, self-assured, and loving. She had one problem, sex.

Hanna grew up in a family as the little princess. She believed the fairy tales about the princess in danger saved by the prince who took care of her forever more. The books she liked. The movies she watched. The family she was from. They were all the same. The woman was a prize that was taken care of. And the man had better appreciate the prize! Hanna in bed was passive. She was the prize that had to be honored, cherished, and served. Afterwards, she insisted on gratitude. Throughout the day, she would insist that she be honored for giving you the prize of her body the night before. She believed that anything that happened was subservient to her great gift of sex. It was frustrating having an argument with her and having her say, "Why are you complaining? You had sex last night."

I started to tell her she had a Prince Charming syndrome. She became mad at my complaining and started to withhold sex. When we did have sex, she would stop after she was satisfied leaving me even more frustrated. The next day she still insisted that I thank her for her gift the night before.

When I left Chicago, we had not made love for four months. For some reason, she still felt we were together. She still considered herself a prize that I had to honor. As I left her, I could see in her face that she still didn't understand how I could let her go.

The eleven months I had been home had been filled with work. The only friends still living around the farm were my parents' friends. Once in a while, they would try to fix me up with a niece or another relative but I still had memories of Hanna so nothing interested me until this fall.

I had gone to town to rent a video for the night. The local TV is sometime pretty bad. During the play-off season, all you might find are local high school and college games. When the local grocery store was out of tapes I was interested in, I went to the video rental store in town. Behind the counter was a cute girl. I asked her where the new releases were. When she answered, I did a double take. Her words were slightly slurred and the vowels were not quite right. I then saw the small hearing aid in her ear. I realized she had to be partially deaf. Not wanting to embarrass her, I went straight to the tapes.

I hadn't gotten out much so I took my time reading the backs of the tapes -- trying to find a video that I hadn't heard of before, which still looked interesting. The girl came up behind me asking if she could help. Startled, I jumped and knocked a dozen video boxes off the shelf. As we put the boxes back on the shelves, I noticed that she had a hearing aid in her other ear and the brightest eyes I had ever seen. They were so sparkly that I never noticed their color that day. I was so flustered after the accident that I picked up the first tape on the shelf and tried to checkout without further embarrassment.

As I gave the girl the two dollars and change for the video, I saw the college textbook on the counter. I had proofread the text three years earlier. Trying to redeem my deflated ego, I asked if she was taking classes for engineering or electronics. I never forgot how her eyes locked onto my face in a penetrating stare.

"Both. How did you know?" she demanded.

Flustered again I fumbled out the words, "Laplacian transforms ... Aren't they used in engineering and electronics?" I pointed to the text, which had the words Laplace and transforms prominently displayed. I escaped the store as fast as I could.

It took me three weeks to get the nerve to go back to the store. Luckily a young man was behind the counter. As I checked out the tapes, I heard the bell on the front door ring. Turning, I saw the girl jog in with a sweat stained athletic shorts and top on. She was built! I could see the bundles of muscles ripple as she moved.

The boy said, "Tabby, could you come in an hour early this evening? I've got a date."

"Okay Joey but you owe me one already. How about trading my Friday shift? I don't like the weekend rush."

"Fine. But if I do trade, you will have to come in two hours early today."

"Deal?"

"Deal."

She turned and saw me staring. She seemed to know what I was looking at. She gave me a silent smile. Turning, she jogged out of the store. Totally embarrassed, I left the store as fast as I could. After that day, I would stop at the video store on Thursdays just to see her. I had learned my lessons from the first two times that I met her. I let her lead the conversations and only opened my mouth the minimum. She was in her twenties. I was in my thirties. I wanted to ask her out but I knew this being a small town the gossip would be hard to take. Instead, we talked about movies and her college classes for fifteen, twenty minutes every time I came in. That was enough for me after my problems with Hanna, girls were unfathomable.

Today I had to see Tabitha just to get Hanna out of my mind.

Chapter 3
Testing

Move-over watched as I got the pickup keys and billfold from my dresser. He gave a yowl as he turned his back. His tail held high, he turned strutting to the front of the house. I knew, when I pulled out of the yard, he would be in the front window watching.

The reason why I was going to town was to see a pretty girl. A couple years back I was proofreading an article by a feminist psychologist about men and girl watching. She ranted and raved about how bad men were and used a mumbo jumbo of big terms to support her ideas. The article was printed. After all, it was just a filler editorial. I knew then what was wrong with her ideas. As I was just a proofreader at that time, no one would listen to me. A basic biological drive of all species is to procreate. It is the only way a species will survive. Its importance, at least in men, is that for an instant of time only one thing is in your mind, the beauty of a woman -- i.e. How capable is her potential to reproduce? Whenever a man sees a woman for the first time, he biologically has to classify her with the unconscious programming in his brain on her fertility. Old women trigger one set of responses, young girls another. The biological response flushes the clutter of thoughts about work, relationships, or watching eyes from the mind for the few seconds you first see the pretty girl. When the clutter comes back, the short break makes it manageable again. Like all things that create brief interludes of happiness, some become addicted. I might be. I don't know. All I do know is that after this last week I need my mind cleaned by a pretty girl. I need an emotional fix caused by the male physiology.

I entered the store with the accompanying clang of the entrance bell. She looked up from the TV playing over the counter and smiled. I nodded and went to the back of the store. The smile worked. I forgot the eyes watching me. I took my time checking the video boxes. I wanted the emotional fix to last as long as possible. I knelt to examine the boxes of a selection of 'B' movies that were kept near the floor. The doorbell clanged and something changed in the store.

A voice said, "All clear. Only the dummy bitch behind the counter."

After a period of silence, another voice said, "Listen Bitch. You just stand still or I'll cut you."

Staying down next to the floor, I eased around the video shelves until I could see the front desk. Two punks with knives were at the counter. One was at the front of the desk waving a switchblade in the air in front of Tabitha's face. The second kid was standing next to Tabitha rummaging in the cash register, a knife blade and bills oozing out of his fists.

The punk in front of the counter said, "The Bitch ain't bad. Let's take her with us."

The one behind the counter answered, "Hell. Robbery is one thing. Snatching a bitch?"

"Sure why not. You've heard her talk. She's a dummy. We just say she wanted it."

The second kid looked her over and slowly a sick grin came to his face. He jabbed Tabitha in the back and shoved her out from behind the counter. From the flinch of pain on Tabitha's face, I knew he had cut her with the knife. The punks started to snicker and give each other congratulatory shoves. Tabitha had walked one step away from the kids while they were busy flattering themselves. I knew I had to do something. From the back of the store, I started to sprint at the boys. Two steps away from them I threw myself into the back of their legs. We all came down in a tangle. I yelled, "Run!" just before my head slammed into the floor.

The next thing I knew I was laying on the floor with groans coming from either side of me. I looked up. Tabitha stood there with the knives in her hand. For an instant, I held my breath. She was beautiful. Face carved in stone. Her hair swept back. A Valkyrie come to life. I turned to the boys next to me on the floor. Both were curled into fetal positions with the hands between their legs withering in pain. The one on my right seemed to be bleeding from the ears.

I backed away from the boys and Tabitha. "I'll call the police," I whispered. At the phone behind the counter, I dialed 911. One of the boys seemed to recover a little and tried to get up. Tabitha kicked him in the stomach so hard he slide a couple of feet across the floor. The boys stayed on the floor until the sheriff's deputy showed up.

When I drove into the yard, Move-over watched as I pulled past the windows of the house. His slitted eyes tracked me to the garage. I went into my workroom. Move-over was already there lying on the old computer his head above the cooling fan.

I got to work on an article by a physicist on a new attempt at a Grand Unification Theory. My hands shook as I touched the keys. At first, my mind wouldn't leave the assault and the police questioning. But one thing about Quantum Mechanics is that you have to concentrate to follow the mathematics. Something about the equations fluttered at the edge of thought. The electromagnetic wave equations looked good. The predicted wave pattern with the addition of a gravity pulse looked interesting ... Something about the nuclear binding forces? What was implied by the equations? If I summarize the starting premises using fuzzy logic algorithms, what would change with...

I woke to knocking at the front door. My head throbbed from lying against the computer chassis. I staggered to my feet. Touching my head, I felt the welt caused by the edge of the computer. Through a window, I saw a large man standing by the door. Living in Chicago for twelve years, makes you cautious. I slipped a wedge under the door when I opened it so it would only move a few inches.

"Hello."

"Mister Daniel Karpinen?" came the stranger's voice.

"Yes." I answered starting to get a little worried.

"Mr. Blythe would like to know if you are alright."

"Mr. Blythe? Who is he?"

"His son was involved in the incident at the video store today. He requested that I stop and see if you needed anything. He is sorry if his son caused you any problems or misunderstandings. He would like you to know that if you need any help to get over this incident you can contact me." He then handed me a card and left. The simple card read 'John W. Jones Attorney at Law' with a phone number at the bottom.

I dropped the card on the table and stumbled into bed. The recoil of my body coming down from the adrenaline rush of the assault at the store had made me groggy. As I fell asleep, I felt safe. I knew that Move-over's eyes were watching.

I woke to the sun streaming through the bedroom window and the force of Move-over jumping on my belly. He purred loudly as he worked his paws back and forth. His needle sharp claws penetrated the blankets, just touching the bare skin between my ribs. Move-over was hungry.

I just finished feeding the cat and pouring myself a glass of orange juice when a faded blue Buick pulled up. A large older man lumbered out of the car and to my door. I waited till he knocked before opening it. He was wrinkled with a day's growth of facial hair. His eyes were puffy from lack of sleep. He reached out his hand and in a tired voice said, "Name's Earl Czeminski. Thank you for helping my daughter."

Still half asleep, I hesitantly shook his hand saying,

"Your welcome sir." I flashed back in years to all the times my father formally shook my hands, graduation, grandma's funeral... I couldn't understand how this man reminded me of my father. My father was a skinny dark man with whipcord speed. This man was large and soft looking with a lumbering movement. By my eighteenth birthday, I could look over my father's head. This man was at least twelve inches taller than me. Then I heard his voice again. My father and this man had grown up here, educated in the local schools, living their lives in this same area. If I closed my eyes, the voice could have been my Dad's.

"Sorry sir. Could you repeat that? I wasn't listening. Yesterday and last night... well I'm still not awake."

He mumbled a little and tried to start his speech a few times before saying, "You need something you ask. Ahhh. And no charge when you come to the store." He was my father. Dad would seldom talk. He would leave that to Ma, but when he did it would burst out of him. If something interrupted him, he would stammer and stutter until he got out just enough to understand what he was saying and then he stopped.

He stayed for a while hemming and hawing, not really knowing what to do or say. We shifted back and forth from one foot to another as his confusion and embarrassment transferred to me. I have never been able to remember what we said to each other for those awkward minutes. Finally, we shook hands again and he left.

With Earl gone, I was alone. I sat drinking my juice. In my mind I saw yesterday again. Tabitha standing over those two boys, chest rising and falling in deep breathes, vital, and alive. And then Earl's voice broke in and changed her into my sister!

I had to do something! Ah yes. Last week I received a paper on the Grand Unification Theory. Really tough math should keep me from thinking. It had been the goal of scientists throughout the ages to find one equation or a single set of related algorithms that would summarize all of physical science. The Unification Theory seemed so close in the 1950's. Electromagnetic waves were summarized in a single equation. Einstein had quantified gravity. Nuclear forces were being examined. And then advancement slowed to a crawl as problems with it continued to plague every new attempt at unification. I could barely understand the simplified versions of the equations the physicist had been using. I knew any stray thoughts in my mind would be forced to leave.

To really work through equations, I would need music. My CD player had a tray that would hold five CD's. I started by putting in something light to get started, Copland. The next three CD's would have to have math music, selections of Mozart, Haydn, Handel, Bach, Pachelbel, and Telemann. The last CD would have to pull me out of the intense math induced trance. Which one to put on? Ah, Bon Jovi.

Fanfare of the Common Man blasted from the stereo speakers as I tried to understand the first set of equations the physicist was using.

One of the problems that any unification theory needed to answer was whether a neutrino had mass and how much. Neutrinos are leftovers. When a nuclear reaction occurs, you have pieces of the atoms and energy released. Some of the energy seemed to disappear. In the 1930's Pauli hypothesized that the missing energy went into a particle. The particle was later called a neutrino by Fermi. It took till 1956 before the first type of neutrino was discovered coming from a nuclear reactor. Neutrinos are so small that they can travel through the earth between atoms never hitting anything. Neutrino detectors are normally put in deep mines just to eliminate the background noise of everyday energy sources. Neutrinos are very very strange.

The problem with neutrinos and mass is that if they have it then all current theories would have to be changed. And the current theories seem to work! If they don't have mass, we don't know where they are going because we seem to be losing them. The detectors are not finding the numbers of certain types of neutrinos we know should be there. If they have mass, we know that the neutrinos are changing to a tau type neutrino, which we can't detect at this time thus explaining the low numbers.

The physicist had taken the current information from both the Super-Kamiokande Experiment and the Sudbury Neutrino Observatory and refined his equations. He had written two equations that were used for two of the types of neutrinos. The equations were identical except for having different constants. The one constant was just a little more than 4.5 times greater than the first. The equations used imaginary numbers in such a way that the neutrinos would disappear from our plane of existence when they had mass. Imaginary numbers are just a technique of math that mimics how real things sometimes turn themselves on and off.

I looked at those equations. They seemed so familiar. The 4.5 times greater and imaginary numbers. 4.5 and imaginary numbers. 4.5 and imaginary numbers. 4.66 and imaginary numbers! Chaos math and Feigenbaum's constant!

This brought to mind three aspects of chaos math. One, all chaos equations with single hump curves bifurcate or split at intervals that are 4.66 apart. Two, chaos type equations are usually written using imaginary numbers because they are easier to solve on computers. And three, there can be relationships between totally different problems if the underlying patterns are the same. In this case, I remember reading in a molecular biology paper, something about types of proteins that would disappear at one site in the cell and reappear as a partial mirror image.

I hurriedly checked the hard drive on my computer and found the biology paper. There sat nearly identical equations. The proteins were doing the same thing as the neutrinos. In this case though the biologist was able to track what had happened and had found a set of ideal conditions. Some of the conditions were found in cells and some were not.

Bach was now playing in the background. On the computer screen I placed both papers side by side. The equations, the music, a pattern, a rhythm, something was there in those sets of equations. My mind blurred as I tried to grasp what I was looking at. Slowly the pounding sounds of Bon Jovi brought me back to now. My head ached. Five hours of math, I needed a break! Just then Move-over yowled for attention.

***

The Chameleon had a plan. Staking out a small rural highway at night, The Chameleon waited for a lone woman to drive by. A specially made focused flashlight rested in the Chameleon's hands.

The prey sang with her radio as she hurried home through the dark night. She had driven for hours and was nearly home. Her thoughts were of family not seen in months. The trap was sprung. A hundred thousand lumens of light hit her dilated eyes. Hands went up trying to shield her from the blinding light. The car swerved. The front tires dropped off the edge of the tarred road. She grabbed the wheel and tried to turn it back on the road. The tires caught on the lip of tar at the edge of the road stopping the front end of the car. The momentum from the back flipped the car into the air. Five times the car turned end over end. The prey had her seatbelt on. She survived but barely conscious. Then the Chameleon came.

The Chameleon had the best technology the Users could provide. Within minutes of searching the prey's purse, the Chameleon had copies of all the documents the prey had. Back at the base, the Chameleon, now a she, made perfect forgeries of the prey's driver license and other papers and photos. She changed everything to reflect her current facade. The forgeries added two inches to her height and subtracted fifteen pounds from her weight. The picture on the driver's license now was hers. With valid identity numbers and proofs, she was ready to infiltrate.

Later that week, she used the prey's credit to purchase a car. On the last day of the week, she entered Chicago from the south. Her first objective would be to find a job.

Chapter 4
Learning

The day was ruined. The arraignment for the two punks took until 5:00. The prosecutor seemed to be just going through the motions. The lawyer for Jordan Blythe and his friend John Jorgenson grilled me for hours trying to get me to make mistakes and correct myself. I finally got fed up with the harassment and called him an idiot, a pea brain. I asked him if the reason he couldn't remember what I said about who had the knife to Tabitha's back was because his elevator didn't go all the way up. That finally got a response from the prosecutor and the judge. I was threatened with contempt. The prosecutor even wanted my comments stricken from the record. I then lectured the lawyer about how he could remember by making a mnemonic out of the letters. The judge in exasperation finally told me I could go. As I left the courtroom, the spectators started to clap. The judge was throwing another hissy fit as I left the room.

The drive home was even worse than the testifying. My brain and body were tired. I swerved onto the shoulder of the road when a large dark shape flashed in front of the windshield. Gulping for air, I looked in the rear view mirror and saw three crows picking at the carcass of some dead animal. I felt picked-over like that animal. I then noticed a bird circling above the road about a hundred yards ahead of the pickup. The hawk stayed circling until I got home and entered the house. There Move-over took over the watching.

"Mr. Blythe?"

"Yes John."

"Both the Czeminski girl and Karpinen testified against your son. I did get both the prosecutor and the judge to agree to a plea bargain. Since both your son and his friend are seventeen, they will have clean records next year. Jorgensen will get sixty days in county jail with probation until he is eighteen and your son will have probation until his eighteenth birthday."

"I thought you said you could make it all go away?"

"I could have if Karpinen and Czeminski hadn't testified."

"No one messes with my family and gets away with it. Hurt them. Hurt them bad. Start with the banks."

"I think the girl has a college loan out. I'll start by having the loan called in. I think it is a federal loan so we will have to have it first transferred to another bank."

"Stop bothering me with the details. You know your job Mister Jones. Just tell me when they are hurting."

***

This was a bad day for the Chameleon. A supervisor just returned from vacation. He was deaf. The Chameleon's disguise worked because she overpowered all the senses. She was an average female secretary. Your nose said she smelled like a woman. Your eyes would say the same. She looked, tasted, walked, talked, and sounded like all the other women in the office. But being an imposter she wasn't quite perfect. The slightly different scent she gave off was offset by her voice. The throaty whisper in her voice could be ignored when contrasted with the popular make-up on her face.

In other words, the supervisor without his sense of hearing to interfere had started watching her with a quizzical look to his face. She knew she had to disappear from this identity and start a new one. She liked the access she had gained by being female. She also noticed that the so-called security that was in place was more interested in her femaleness than in what she did. The Chameleon had heard talk about a lesbian bar downtown. She would go there. It should be easy to attract a new prey to exchange identities with. A new prey to destroy and place her current identification with. A new prey to be used to camouflage her infiltration.

Her change of identity was easier than she imagined. She had dressed the prey with her clothing and purse, destroyed her face and hands by leaving her body on the train tracks. The changes the Chameleon had to make to fit the new prey's identity were minor, slightly different shade of skin tone and hair color. This prey had a better education than the last. The Chameleon could infiltrate the community at a higher level.

***

Air on a G-String by Bach was playing in the background and I was looking again at the Grand Unification equations. I had proofed the article and sent it back to the office the day before but I couldn't stop thinking about the electromagnetic equations.

I had decided to put the equations away but something made me look at them again using fuzzy logic. Fuzzy logic assumes that you don't have accurate information. A strange thing happens when you assume inaccuracy. You can process more information with more accuracy than with common math, but it only works better on real life problems. I could still remember the first fuzzy math problem I proofed.

A college math professor had his class write out the problem of when he would get to his office if he left home at 7:10 in the morning. The class spent 3 weeks timing the traffic lights and examining his morning route. They then wrote out the problem using standard mathematical methods and fuzzy logic. Using standard math, he would arrive at his office at 7:44 plus or minus 8.5 minutes. Using fuzzy logic, he would arrive at his office at approximately 7:48. The rest of the semester the class recorded the arrival time of the professor. Except for 3 arrivals, the professor walked into his office within the 8.5 minutes of 7:44 but for 3/4ths of the arrival times he arrived within 2 minutes of 7:48.

Fuzzy logic had the more accurate answer because it accepts the fact that the things are never exact. The professor might leave home at 7:11 one day but the traffic lights will average the later time of that one-day so he still arrives at 7:44. Fuzzy logic balances the inaccuracies by acknowledging that they are there. The more variations in a problem the greater the accuracy using fuzzy logic.

A Japanese mathematician had taken a set of algorithms designed by a logician by the name of Kosko and applied them to radio transmissions. I had run across his article in *Scientific American* while proofing a story from IBM Labs on a new system of transmitting information between computers without using cables. Since radio waves are electromagnetic, I used the mathematician's algorithms on the Unification equations. And then it happened! Right there on the computer screen! The equations showed that just like the neutrinos electromagnetic radiation could convert to mass with gravity. You could use radio waves to make gravity!

The conversion to gravity was so small that it was unnoticeable, but it was there in the equations. I started playing with the numbers on the screen. The equations stayed the same. I tried different combinations. Still the conversion to gravity was so small you couldn't even find it let alone use it. Suddenly a spike appeared in the numbers. Harmonics of different frequencies could add up to make noticeable gravity.

I stared at the computer screen. Silence. I don't know how long I watched the same string of numbers. But Move-over stretched up my leg, inserted his claws through the fabric of my pants, and yowled. It was morning. He wanted food. I had worked through the night.

I suddenly had to empty my bladder. The twelve hours sitting in front of a computer screen had made inroads in the balance between my kidney output and my bladder capacity. I ran to the bathroom to the accompaniment of my growling stomach and Move-over's hungry cries. During the long minutes standing in front of the toilet, I wondered if I actually found a way of making artificial gravity. Then I started to laugh. I laughed so hard I missed the stool. Wiping up the small puddle next to the toilet, I kept hearing the comment from an imaginary reporter that started my laughter. "Sir, what was the first thing you did after you realized you discovered artificial gravity?"

The muscles in my lower abdomen hurt from the pressure of my over extended bladder and laughter. I slowly finished cleaning and limped to the kitchen. I needed to replace my fluids! I was on my second glass of orange juice when I fell asleep.

Bang, bang, bang. I didn't want to move but the pounding continued. I tried to wake, but failed. I tried again and succeeded in lifting my head. I watched the warm glass of orange juice for a while. Then I saw Move-over staring at me from the other side of the kitchen table. Finally, I focused on the front door and the knocking coming from it. I started to answer the door but had to turn back to set the glass back on the kitchen table. When I got to the door, it had turned quiet. For an instant, I stopped to wonder why the door had stopped making noise. Opening the door, I saw a figure walking away.

"Yes" I croaked out.

The figure turned. It was Tabitha. "Hi, I thought no one was home." She walked closer. A grin came to her face. "You must keep late hours." Before I could say anything, her face turned serious and she continued, "With the cops, lawyers, and everything else I never got a chance to thank you." After a pause, "Thank you."

"Come in. I'm still half-asleep. I'll make coffee."

When she hesitated, I said, "Come on. I need to wake-up and the coffee's not going to get made standing out here."

The grin came back to her face. "If you don't mind me saying so... You look like hell."

"I've been busy."

"With what?"

I had to tell someone about what I had found, someone who would understand. "I think I just discovered a way to make artificial gravity."

"Sure you did... You're serious!"

The next hours were more fun than I had in years. I explained what I had done and showed her the equations and computer predictions. The computer room is crowded when two chairs are put in front of the screen. I could feel her excitement, her movement, and smell her scent. It was stimulating. It was erotic.

Suddenly she turned. Her face was alive. "Let's build it and see if it works?"

"Let's!"

She grabbed me and hugged. For the first time in my life I melted into another's arms. I held her till she stopped moving. I finally forced myself away. I looked at her face. It was soft now with a hint of moistness around her eyes. I finally took a deep breath. "Let's make a list. We need to span as much of the electromagnetic spectrum as we can. The equations show that we need a broad band of frequencies for it to work."

"Yes a list."

Chapter 5
Experimenting

I needed to get outside after spending the last few weeks' proofreading and working on artificial gravity. This is northern Minnesota so I loaded number 7 birdshot in my father's old Harrington single-shot shotgun to carry. I wasn't planning on using the gun, but for walking through the woods it is expected to carry something -- a saw, an axe, a gun, or a camera.

The morning was beautiful. Ice fog covered the land. The trees, grasses, and buildings were frosted. The morning light penetrated the low-lying clouds reflecting off the frosted ground in sparkles of pink and blue. The ground was slightly warmer than the ice fog so the mist stopped about five feet from any objects. If I squatted down, I could see clearly the forest line across the field. The frosted grass crunched with every step. Every breath I took was fresh and clean. Frost formed on my eye lashes and nose hairs. By the time I reached the logging road at the end of the field, I was in heaven.

The farm's woods were crisscrossed with trails wide enough for a tractor pulling a wood cart. I entered the maze grateful to be lost for a while. In the corner of the woods, a red oak had blown over a few years back during a storm. My father and I had cut the broken tree into firewood but we had left the shattered stump. When I had moved back home this last summer, I had taken my chainsaw and carved the stump into a chair. That was my first goal for the day. I sat on the cold wood. Closed my eyes. And listened to the soft sounds of the forest.

When Tabitha and I started the project, we knew we would need a base to build the contraption on. My father, like all old time farmers, had an equipment graveyard behind the fields in the woods. There were three cars, two Alice-Chalmers tractors, and a 1953 Ford truck stripped and rusting in between the trees. The vehicles had given their parts to keep the other farm equipment working. We pulled the empty transmission case from an old Dodge and mounted it on blocks in the garage.

We needed to concentrate the waves so the first thing we did was buy a satellite dish and mount it on the face of the transmission. We would have trouble adjusting frequencies in the light range so we began by buying four identical laser pointers. Mounting them on the edge of the transmission case with bolts and clamps we lined them up so their beams met at the focus of the dish.

If you throw two rocks in a pond, you will see that the waves on the surface will interfere with each other. They will build up in spots and disappear in others. We wanted the electromagnetic waves to build at the focus until they collapsed and became gravity. From my work, I knew that certain frequency ratios like 3:1, 5:2, 4:1, 2:1, and 7:2 were unstable. I also knew that other ratios like 1:1 and 3:2 combinations were stable. Using the frequency of the lasers as a starting point, we mounted radio transmitters in the stable frequencies that would broadcast into the dish. I talked the local phone-company into selling an outdated microwave transmitter to me and Tabitha borrowed an infrared unit from the college. Before we could start testing, we needed at least one more microwave transmitter and two more in the radio broadcast range.

Tabitha had gone to see what else she could get from her college and to clear up some problems she had with her financial aid so I had taken the day off. When I opened my eyes, I knew what I would see. Three feet away a red squirrel stood on his haunches watching. In a near by tree, two nuthatches hunted for food. They took turns. One watched while the other fed.

The air became warmer, but the fog didn't lift. It thickened and settled closer to the ground. Without the frost, the damp leaves made no noise when I walked. In a silent blanket, I wondered through the woods. The only sounds I heard were the rustling of the small animals that watched. From memory, I threaded my way back home. Nearing the edge of the woods, I stopped. The nuthatches fluttered in front of me. They settled on a near by tree. One looked off to the edge of the woods and the other glanced back and forth between his mate and me. I followed the bird's gaze. Slowly out of the mist, I made out the back of a man. He was watching the farm buildings.

"Is there something I can help you with?"

The man jumped. Dropping his binoculars, he stood nervously looking at me. As he tried to clear his throat to make a reply, I could see him glance at the old shotgun I had in my hands.

"Just walking in the woods... I got turned around in the fog." He turned sideways to me and pointed past the buildings. "Is that county road 26?"

"Yes."

"Thanks."

He headed off across the fields. I walked over to where he had been standing. The grass and leaves were dry. He had to have been standing there for hours watching the farm. What was going on?

***

The Chameleon loved this planet. Unlike most intelligent species the one here had very little herd or family organization. This species consisted of individuals with only a visage left of family units and the herd had fragmented into strange overlapping groupings. Regional herds were fragmented by national, which were then fragmented by state and various local communities. Then overlapping herds made up of religious and social groups spread across the large territorial groupings, making a mesh of competing loyalties. That meant the Chameleon only had to deal with one individual at a time. She was more than a match for anyone she had encountered.

She did to the people she encountered what her Users did to the worlds they savaged. She learned everything she could about the person. Swindled what she could from them and stole the rest. She used five people since she took her last prey. Her bank account now numbered in the millions of dollars. There again she thought, "What a wonderful planet!" Money was such an anonymous way to calculate success here.

The Chameleon would start her new job today, executive vice president. The old vice president had been her lover until she doctored the books and told his wife about the affair. Her new office had just been refurbished. After all, you can't just scrub clean brains, blood and bullet a hole after a suicide. Great Users! She loved this planet. Maybe she would retire here. It was so fun.

Chapter 6
Response

Leena had trouble sleeping. The bed was cold. She had sent her husband Fred to sleep on the couch after she heard about his helping Blythe and Jones mess with the Czeminskis' bank accounts.

Leena had had a crush on Earl Czeminski in high school. He was so tall and his legs looked so good in his basketball shorts. Martha was a cheerleader and had the inside track with Earl but Leena just couldn't help fantasizing about Earl's long legs and butt during each basketball game. She never regretted marrying Fred but she always had a soft spot for Earl. She was furious with Fred for helping those out-of-towners, Blythe and Jones, hurt Earl and his family. Fred was the president of the bank. He should have stood up to Blythe and Jones even if Blythe had the most money in the bank. Fred knew that he personally would take care of Earl's financial problems or he wasn't going to get back into bed anytime soon.

Leena decided she would call Olga in the morning before the first soaps started. Oggie would know how to handle outsiders.

"Oggie?"

"Leena. Did you catch the end of *Hospital*? I think Julie is going to leave Spencer."

"You're, kidding. Is she going after Carlos?"

"I think so."

"Oggie, do you remember Earl Czeminski?"

"Oh, yes. He had great legs. I loved the way his ass looked when he bent over bouncing the ball before a free throw."

"Well, that rich guy Friedrick Blythe and his lawyer Johnny Jones have it in for Earl."

"You're kidding! Why?"

"You know about those kids trying to rob the video store a couple of weeks ago."

"Ya."

"The girl that stopped them was Earl's daughter Tabitha and the boy that helped was Danny Karpinen, Hazel's boy. Wellll, it was Blythe's son, Jordan, with the Jorgenson brat who tried to rob the place. Blythe wants to get back at Tabitha and Danny.

"My Fred told me that Blythe and Jones said they would pull their money out of the bank unless he called in all the loans the Czeminskis had. Fred pulled the loans but I told him he had to fix things or he would be sleeping on the couch for the next year."

"Good for you. My Tom better not be helping Blythe or he won't be doing any sheriffing in my bedroom. I'll make sure that Tom will spread the news to the other deputies to keep an eye out for any dirty tricks by Blythe or Jones."

"Ya ... Uknow, Oggie. I think Julie is pregnant with Mitch's child."

"Damnit. I knew I should have taped *Days* yesterday..."

***

"Erma?"

"Sylvia?"

"Yes. Just got off the phone with Oggie. Did you hear Mitch got Julie pregnant?"

"You're kidding, Mitch? I thought it would have been Bruce."

"And did you know about Blythe making trouble for Earl?"

"Not Legs Czeminski!"

"Yup, Legs. And he is also going after Hazel's son, Dan."

"Goddamnit, Syl. We godda do something about that..."

***

"Emma, this is Betty again. I just got off the phone with Eleanor. She talked to Zoe, Stella, and Fran. With Helga, Johanna, Marta, and Gretta we will have enough votes to pull the investments of our Coffee Klutch Club from Blythe's company. Gertrude said her Al will take care of placing the new investments.

"Did you hear what Margrete did when she heard about Jeff helping Blythe?"

"What?"

"She grabbed him by the nuts and hauled his ass outside. She yelled at him for twenty minutes. Someone called the cops because Leena's Tom showed up. Tom got things settled down."

"That sounds like Marg. Do you remember the time in tenth grade when she found out David was seeing Sylvia on the side?"

"Oh, yes. David couldn't walk straight for a week and Syl still doesn't talk to Marg."

"Julie left Spencer and moved in with Carlos."

"Damn. Blythe made me miss *Hospital*. He's going to pay for that..."

***

John W. Jones was worried. Friedrick Blythe was not a man to take bad news lightly. By now Earl Czeminski should have been trying to sell his assets. The video store closed. The small laundromat should have a 'for sale' sign in the window. And he should have been laid off his job at the electric co-operative.

This was crazy. Fred at the bank was putting off talking to him. Jeff at the co-operative stopped accepting his calls. And his local contact in the prosecutor's office had said that she wasn't going to be giving him any more information. He still had the local prosecutor in his pocket but the judge was starting to act hinky. Plus, it seemed that Blythe's companies had become a take-over target for some Wall Street investor. Jones was trying to stem the losses while finding out which investment firm was organizing the raid. But the biggest stock sale hadn't come from New York. It was some small Midwest company he couldn't track down that was incorporated under the strange name of Coffee Klutch Club.

God. It was only a half-hour before his next meeting with Blythe. He couldn't even give Blythe something on Daniel Karpinen. His employer was in Chicago and the company was large enough that Jones hadn't found any leverage that would work with the company to get him fired.

Chapter 7
Fizzle

It was the Christmas holidays and Tabitha and I were finally ready to test out our contraption. We worked for hours in the old garage so we could finish testing the setup before she had to leave for the start of the next semester in January. Tabitha said her financial problems were finally straightened out.

The old garage was cold so I dragged in an old propane salamander to keep the edge off while we were working. The salamander was able to hold the temperature just warm enough so we could work without our gloves and jackets. The old cement floor never got warm from the heater. I layered a dozen old gunnysacks around the Dodge transmission to cushion the concrete and keep the cold back. My legs just couldn't handle the hours of kneeling on the cement without the layers of burlap.

The salamander had been running for an hour. Our breath stopped making steam and we started to sweat. Taking off my jacket, I snatched a quick look at Tabby while she shrugged off hers. The fabric of her shirt pulled tight as she wiggled free. God was she built!

We triple checked the connections. The satellite dish was bolted firmly to the Dodge transmission. The four laser pointers were as close as we could get to the focus of the dish. We had five radio transmitters placed around the outside of the dish using the dish to reflect the signals to the focus. The two microwave and one infrared transmitters were balanced between the other units along the edge of the dish. We backed away, shaded our eyes and turned the switch on.

Nothing happened.

I rocked the switch back and forth a few times. Still nothing happened.

I looked at Tabitha. She looked at me. A smile formed on her face. Giggles started and full belly laughs followed. We hung on to each other, sides hurting, legs wobbling, trying to keep from peeing.

Through the laughter I felt Tabby's muscles move. Still laughing, I wanted to feel more. My hands went beneath her flannel shirt. Her hands unbuckled my pants. We rolled onto the gunnysacks, clothes pulled apart, laughing. Our skin felt so warm compared to the cold of the garage. We pressed ourselves together reveling in the warmth. The course weave of burlap rubbed the skin where her warm flesh didn't touch. The laughter stopped as the burlap rubbed my knees raw and started again when we finished.

We pulled our clothes together, turned the salamander off, and ran to my bedroom. Clothes went flying again but this time there was no laughter. I watched every move her body made as we rolled and moved in time with each other. It was much later. Tabitha was asleep. I was watching small droplets of sweat roll down her body around her breasts. Every droplet took a different path. I blew on her bare chest watching the goosebumps change the direction of the droplets. That was it! The equations showed that every electromagnetic transmission had to be at an exact frequency and at an exact nexus. Our contraption couldn't be exact. Just the changes in air temperature would sift the transmissions. I would have to fuzz the transmitters so they would cover a small band of frequencies close to what we needed. That way they would combine when, by chance or chaos, everything matched the frequencies we wanted.

I blew again on her bare skin. This time not only did goosebumps form but her nipples hardened. A pair of arms grabbed me and pulled me in.

I woke first and slipped out of bed. I started to tiptoe out of the bedroom until I saw the two hearing aids on the headboard. I felt eyes on my naked body. I looked at sleeping Tabitha. Eyes shut. Move-over was on a dresser top lying upside down and stretched out. His slitted eyes glowed from under his nose and between his dangling front paws.

"Move-over, you old voyeur. Did you get an eyeful?"

I dressed and went to the garage. I had an idea about running the output from an old boombox into the transmitters to fuzzy the signals. I was just bolting the boombox to the Dodge transmission when the door opened.

"There you are? I was wondering where you ran off to."

"I had an idea about the signals. I think we need to fuzz them a little."

"I get it. The frequencies aren't matching but since we can't increase the accuracy we fuzz the frequencies so they will occasionally match up.

"What would you like me to do?"

"I need a number 8 bolt with a nut that is about one inch long. There should be a few in the box over there."

I started to hear humming and the tinkling of bolts and nuts. I looked over to Tabitha. The box was on the floor. She was bent at the waist, hands deep in the box with her legs spread wide. Her ass was rotating in time with the tune she was humming. God did she have a well-built set of legs and ass. I walked up behind her slowly touching her moving body with mine. We never got back to finishing our contraption before she left for school.

Tabitha was back in school. I have my work. I have the contraption we were making. And I have Move-over. But the house still felt empty. Looking out the window, I saw the clear sunlit cold of sub zero weather. Putting on my wools, I got the green wax tin and my skis from the back entryway. The waxing took just a minute and I was out the door heading across the snow to the woods across the fields.

One hundred yards from the house the coordinated hand leg movements of cross-country skiing broke through the feeling of loneliness. I was alert and ready to see the woods. By seeing, I meant more than seeing. I was ready to become, like my Uncle Ben, a part of the woods not just a viewer of the woods. Winter was the only time I could become part of the woods. During the other seasons, there was just too much life. I could only blend in. Halfway to the forest, I stopped and closed my eyes. I listened to the wind and rustling of the few dry leaves that hadn't fallen off the trees. My breathing slowed matching that of the forest. I headed on.

It had been a week since the last snow and I could see all of the activity that had happened since then. Mice, deer, dogs, rabbits, wolves. Just inside the tree line I came upon three depressions with the flaring marks of wings. Three partridges had slept last night within sight of the farmhouse. Rabbit tracks were just a dozen yards farther. I stopped to look for the rabbit's black eye. I found it thirty feet to the right. Squinting in the bright sun, I made out the white outline of the rabbit against the snow. In the winter the woods are thick with life. And the tracks tell you the patterns of the living.

I got to the stump chair. Brushing off the snow, I thought about the change in the pattern of my life Tabitha made. There was a throbbing in my hand. The puukko Ben had given me was there. I didn't remember taking it out but the rocking of the balanced blade between my fingers gave the knife the feel of a heartbeat. I looked. A nuthatch and two chickadees were watching. I put the knife away and warmed my frozen fingers between my legs. What did the watching mean?

***

The Chameleon had a pleasant surprise with the new position. She was in charge of the corporate spies that the company used. Most of the spies worked for the magazines run by the company. It was strange but some of the companies seemed to expect and even work with the spies. One of the magazines would have spy pictures of the newest automobile designs with written articles that included quotes from the spied upon automobile company executives. This place was so much like the Users; she might just have to recommend that a permanent colony be placed here.

***

Jones finally had something for Blythe. He hired a track student to injure the Czeminski girl. The student was to foul the girl during next track meet so Blythe could watch it happen. The detective he hired to find something on Karpinen was still having trouble. There was no easy way to observe the farmhouse he lived in. There was just too much open space in the country. The phone taps were not helping. There were few calls being made and except for a few odd email messages the Internet access was encrypted. The detective was able to break the codes but they were difficult enough that they were broken after the materials Karpinen was working on were publicly published. Jones knew he needed to make more happen to the Czeminskis and Karpinen soon or he would be looking for a new job.

***

Tabitha rushed for the bus. There were twenty other athletes already aboard. It was a record for the college. Twenty invited to the pre-season invitational track meet in the Twin Cities. It was the third time Tabitha made it to the invitational. She settled back into the seat to sleep the hours to the arena. The noise from the first-timers was just a faint background hum to soother her to slumber.

-48-

***

The limo pulled up to the arena fifteen minutes before the start of the meet. Jones had made sure that prime seats were saved for him and Blythe in the half full athletic center. Blythe had been occupied with financial reports during the flight down and had said only a dozen words to Jones. Nervous, Jones led Blythe to their seats. Praying that everything would go well, he told Blythe that the 3000-meter race was scheduled seventh in the line-up.

"This is your last chance Jones. If this doesn't work, you will be looking for a new job. Anything on Karpinen yet?

"Have you found leverage?"

"No, but I have arranged for a fire to take place at Czeminski's laundromat this weekend."

"Why haven't you got something on Karpinen?"

"The company he works for is too big and he is too important to their operations for an attack on that front. He spends most of his time at home and with this being winter I can't get someone close to the farm he lives on without the possibility of being seen. You told me you wanted whatever happened to him to occur without someone tracing it back to us. To do that in the winter, we would have to go out-of-house and hire a professional fixer. You said you wanted to keep things in-house for now.

"Sir, the 3000 meters is about to start. The dark hair girl running next to Czeminski is the one I hired from her school. To play it safe, I also hired the blonde two lanes over. They were told to take her out on the second lap on the curve right in front of us."

They watched in silence as the race started. Czeminski was third through the first lap. On the backstretch of the second lap, the blond pulled along side her. The corner came. The blonde stumbled and fell into Czeminski. They both fell on the track with the blonde's legs tangled with Czeminski's. The brunette was running right behind the two. She clumsily tried to jump the tangle but landed on

Czeminski's legs. They could hear the crack of the bone breaking from the stands.

"Good. You finally did something right, Jones."

The two men left the meet and got into the waiting limo for the drive to the airport for the flight back.

Chapter 8
Pop

I was making the finishing touches to the contraption under Move-over's watchful eyes. The cat had climbed up into the rafters of the garage. Every so often, I would hear soft feet rustling the junk stored between the rafters or see dust dropping to the garage floor. I would look up to see Move-over's eyes glowing from overhead. The cat seemed to have a way of dropping dust so it would get into my nose. Other than the old boombox, the most noticeable change I made to the contraption was writing CONTRAPTION on the side of the transmission using a can of Alice Chalmers orange spray paint.

I heard the door open behind me.

"I see you decided to name it."

"Tabitha! What are you doing here? I was going to drive up and see you this weekend."

She stepped into the garage. I could see the split trouser leg and the walking cast that went up to her knee. "I had a little accident and took the rest of the week off."

"What happened?"

"Not much. During the 3,000 meter invitational a runner from St. Cloud State tripped into me on a corner and a teammate ran into both of us."

"Sit down... Does it hurt... Do you need anything... What can I do?"

The laughter came. Gasp. "Yes." Gasp. "Stop making meee laugh."

She was okay. And even with the cast she was sexy. She knew immediately what I was thinking. It could have been the memory of what happened the first time we laughed together or the bulge in my pants.

"You just hold it there buddy. I want to see this contraption work before I let you scratch under my cast or anyplace else."

It only took a few more minutes to finish checking the circuits. I lifted Tabby on the workbench and climbed up to sit beside her. We had a little countdown before flipping the switch. At first, nothing happened except for giggles, but then I saw a slight ripple near the focus of the reflector dish.

"Did you see that?"

"It looks sort of like the ripples from a stove burner. I wonder if it is hot."

Meow. There was Move-over walking along the two by six rafter. A large dust bunny fell from his feet. Slowly it drifted to the Contraption.

Pop.

The circuit breakers blew. The garage plunged to dark with the only light coming from a small north window. I ran to the electrical box and flipped the lights back on. The contraption was in pieces. The bolts holding the transmitters in place were pulled loose. The dish was pulled off the Dodge transmission. Most of the pieces were dangling from their wires. The rest were lying on the garage floor.

"I'll be damned. It worked."

The only incident to mar the day happened much later. Tabitha was lying naked on my bed after having me scratch her toes and the flesh around the top of the cast. I, of course, took the opportunity to scratch the rest of her body numerous times. After scratching for the tenth time the skin under the top edge of the cast, I was running my fingers up the inside of her thigh.

"That tickles." She jerked her leg up. Since my head was between her knees at the time, the cast connected with my nose.

Later, I was in the bathroom pulling dried red toilet paper from my nose watching my eyes raccoon up from the bruises when I started to laugh.

"Dan, what's so funny?"

"Tabby, do you remember me telling you about when I figured out the equations?"

"Yes. You said that you had been working ten hours straight so you ran to the bathroom. You started laughing because if a reporter asked..." She hit me. "You are not going to tell anyone about what happened."

***

Jones yawned. It was 3:00 am. He couldn't leave his office until he knew everything happened as planned. He jerked spilling the cold cup of coffee he had in his hands. His office was only three blocks from the fire station. The fire siren was loud enough to wake sleeping volunteers at the outskirts of town. It was nearly deafening at three blocks. Walking to the window, he saw the orange glow from the location of the laundromat. Satisfied he left for home and bed.

Tuesday morning and things were not well. The fire gutted the laundromat but Jones wasn't able to get suspicion for the arson to be placed on Earl Czeminski. On Monday, He had tried a little pressure on the DA to look into the fire but the DA came back with the news that the police were sure that Czeminski wasn't involved and that they had suspects that they were looking into. When Jones asked the DA who the suspect was, the DA refused to tell him.

The investment drain in Blythe's companies had gained the notice of at least two Wall Street take-over specialists and the work to keep control of the companies had turned into a free-for-all. It was time to go outside for help. He had contacted a shady investigating firm known for their dirty tricks. He had to convince Blythe to go with the firm. Jones needed deniability if things went wrong and professional help in finding out who was raiding their companies.

Jones left his office. Walked down the hall to Blythe's.

"Sherry, I need to speak to the boss."

"Sorry, Mr. Jones but he said not to let anyone in until he finished this call."

"I'll wait."

Ten minutes later. "He is off the phone." Sherry picked up the phone and pressed the intercom. "Mr. Jones is here... Okay sir. Wait one more minute and then go in."

"Mr. Blythe. I need help. I'm a lawyer. I know how to handle things after they happened. It is this setting up of things before that is giving me problems. We have this detective firm looking into Karpinen. I would like to expand their duties to include Czeminski and the other work."

"We can't control an outside firm."

"Sir, I thought of that. I can funnel everything through a third party. I will hire a lawyer friend and use attorney/client privilege to block the connection between us and the detective firm."

"Don't you mean you and the detective firm?"

"Yes, me. This will also help with our financial problems. I haven't had the time to really look into stopping these corporate raiders while working on Czeminski and Karpinen."

"How much..."

Jones made it through with his job still intact. It was the toughest sell job he had with Blythe. He decided that it was time to start looking for a new job. He was flying out to New York tomorrow. He would just float his resume while he worked on saving Blythe's companies. People were always looking for good corporate lawyers who didn't mind getting their hands a little dirty. The only problem was that you didn't have job security. But Jones decided that all he needed was another five more years in the trenches and he would have enough in his Swiss bank accounts to retire and live off the interest.

***

Tabitha continued crying in my arms. My shirt was soaked through. It was both scary and comforting to hold her. I stroked her back slowly. There was no sexual desire in my hands but there still was a thrill of touching her warmth. Through gaps between the tears, she told how the family's laundromat had been torched and the loan and banking problems that were started by Blythe and Jones. My mind went back to the man watching my home. Could he have been working for Blythe? I looked up and saw Move-over's eyes. I silently whispered, "You need to watch her."

"Meowwwerrr." Somehow I knew Move-over understood and had accepted the task.

Tabitha left my arms to wash her face. The whole side of my shirt was wet and cold. I went to the bedroom to put on a new shirt. Talking through the walls and doors to Tabitha, "You don't have to go back to school. You can stay here."

"I am going to school. Blythe isn't going to stop me from finishing my degree."

"You need to be careful. If Blythe had the laundromat burned, your broken leg might not have been an accident."

"I thought of that myself. I will find out what happened."

She came out of the bathroom. Her face was the same one I saw those weeks earlier in the video store. I knew she would find out what had happened. But I was still afraid. I spent the remaining hours of the weekend trying to talk her into letting me protect her or to play it safe and stay home. She refused both choices.

I was again sitting on the stump in the woods. The knife blade throbbing in my hand and the birds watching. This time when I had skied into the woods, I had taken a step further in the transformation. I had become a predator. I felt the forest breathing and the life but this time my senses went out to find the life and my body relaxed to attack. At first, I couldn't understand why the tension left my limbs and my skiing rhythm changed to a liquid flow. But there was a clatter as two tree limbs connected in the breeze. My body flowed into readiness before my senses could classify the sound. I had not realized the body had to relax before it could fight.

I had to protect Tabitha. I had to protect myself. Damnit. I needed to learn how to do both. The puukko flew from my hands and stuck one inch into a tree trunk equal distance between two nuthatches who were watching me. The nuthatches didn't fly away or stop their watching. I skied to the tree and pulled the knife from the wood. The birds finally flew to the next tree when I got within arm's reach.

***

Jones had spent two days with the bankers. Jones knew his actions had given them a breathing spell of at least a few months. His next meeting was with Finkelstien, Bradly and Associates. It was a small investment firm that Jones had worked with before. He had gone to college with Harry O'Bradly.

"Harry O. You really should put the O back in your name."

"Johnny, you know how Wall Street is. I had to leave Finkelstien's name on the company just so I could stay in business. No one except you would hire a firm named O'Bradly to do their investing.

"Enough small talk. You look worried Johnny. What do you need?"

"Raiders are going after my boss's companies. I think I might be a casualty of the take over attempt. I need to get my investments liquid enough so I can pull out without loosing too much money. Plus I would like to find out who is going after Blythe."

"Okay, Johnny. There are some short terms bonds we

can use..."

"Now that is finished, what can you tell me about Coffee Klutch?"

"Coffee Klutch? How are they involved?"

"They started the problems by pulling out their investments in mass. Blythe's market value dropped 30 points in one day."

"You're in trouble. The Coffee Klutch started investing in the early 80s. They are a private investment firm but all the big boys started watching them closely in the 90s. They have never had a negative year. They are damn good. If they have lost faith in Blythe, there is a better than 50/50 chance that nothing you try will save you."

"Just who is Coffee Klutch? I've never heard of them and I can't find any details about them."

"They are a private investment club so not much is known. I do know that they started out with 10,000 dollars and their current portfolio is over 375 million. For years I thought the Coffee Klutch was a group of Ivy League graduates. You know what I'm talking about. A group of friends just graduating from college put up 1,000 dollars each and go into the market. But a few years back I was drinking with a friend I have in the FCC. A news program about investing on Wall Street come on the bar's TV and this being the financial district no one turned it off. The reporters had a monkey picking stocks. The monkey out performed most of the big firms. The monkey even outperformed me for three-quarters. The news show went on to a group of little old ladies investing in the market. That is when my friend whispered, "The Coffee Klutch is the same thing.""

That is when everything fell into place for Jones. The downtown dinner with the name the Coffee Clutch. The side room reserved every Tuesday night for the ladies of the town. The town had turned against Blythe. With 375 million in the stock market, they could do what they wanted. It now made sense. The banker not following instructions. The problems getting the DA and police to do what he wanted. It was time to get out.

"Harry, Blythe is going down. He has maybe six months before he looses his companies. I want you to pull all of my stocks out of his companies. But I need it done slowly and quietly so he doesn't know that I am quitting. How long do you think it will take?"

"How much money are you willing to lose in the deal?"

"As little as possible."

"Give me four months. To make this work you will need to make sure he doesn't suspect you are leaving."

"He won't."

Chapter 9
Eyes

I finished an article on the affect of deforestation on local water tables. I encrypted the story and emailed it to the home office. Move-over was watching me from the top of the computer case. Since he had to have his head on the computer's cooling fan and the fan was in back of the case, he was trying a new method of lying on the computer. He was on his back with his head coming out from under his shoulder. I scratched his chin. The cat's rumbling was three times louder than the old muffin fan on the computer. Just audible over the purring was the thrashing of the computer's hard drive.

I wondered if Blythe had someone trying to hack into my files. What about my work on gravity? The best way to protect something is not to protect it. I decided to send copies of my equations to every college and lab that I had email addresses to. If everyone had it with my name on it, no one could steal the information.

The sending of the emails took the rest of the morning. I needed to get away from the computers. I had work to do on the Contraption. I bought a new reflector dish. The dish was the only thing that seemed to be broken beyond repair. To protect the dish during the next test, I was welding steel straps to the Dodge transmission case. The straps were long enough to reach the dish. I would bend each strap to form a harness around the outside edge of the dish. I lost myself in the blue arch of the electric welder. Tomorrow I would start assembling a frame to mount the electromagnetic transmitters on. I was going to use inch and a quarter galvanized steel water pipes. The pipes were overkill for the frame but my dad had a stack of them left from the waterlines we had for the stock tanks.

All the work I was doing didn't stop the worries about Tabitha. Would she be alright?

***

It took all week but Tabitha finally got Sue alone. "Suzie, I noticed something strange when you ran into me. You did it on purpose. I want to know why."

"You're paranoid. I never meant to hurt you. Let me go!"

Tabitha walked Suzie into the corner of the dead end hallway. "Talk to me."

"Get away. You're crazy."

"Maybe, but you are going to tell me what happened."

"Please. Please let me go."

"Talk."

Tabitha pressed into Suzie holding her against the wall. After a few minutes something broke within and Suzie's shoulders dropped, tears came. "So much money. I needed the money. I didn't think. I didn't ... not until I felt your leg break. God, why did I do it?"

"Who gave you the money?"

"Some guy. I don't know. He seemed to know I was broke. He gave me five hundred dollars in cash. A week later he came with another five hundred and said he wanted you hurt, bad enough so you would be out for the season. A thousand dollars. More than enough money to finish the year. But then he said he wanted it done during a meet. I said no way. But he showed me another five hundred. He left. He said he would come back in a week.

"When he came back, he told me the plan. How you would be knocked down and I would fall on top. It didn't seem real. I didn't want it to be real. He was willing to give me a thousand dollars more. I wanted that money..."

Tabitha left Suzie standing at the end of the hall.

***

Ever since Jones got back from New York, he felt peoples' eyes on him. The older waitress at the dinner seemed to glare as she filled his coffee cup. Two sheriff's deputies came in and took a corner booth. Between sips of coffee, they would look across the dinner at him. Fred from the bank came in and sat at a table near the cops. Jones overheard the waitress say to Fred, "Leena would be proud of you standing up to them."

Jones had to protect himself. He had to do Blythe's bidding until he got as much of his money as he could out of Blythe's companies. But he had to also keep up the dirty tricks on Czeminski and Karpinen. How was he going to do both with everyone watching?

"Excuse me. Mr. Jones."

"What? Sorry, I was thinking about some work back at the office. What can I do for you officer?"

"Oh nothing, I saw you studying your coffee so intently. I thought that something might be bothering you. Something you might want to tell me. But if it is just office work, I will leave you to it. You can't believe how much paperwork we have to do every day."

The waitress came and topped off his coffee. "Tom. Say hi to Oggie for me."

"I will. Good coffee today Fran."

"Mr. Jones, do you want anything else?"

"No. Just coffee. Thanks."

***

Late Friday afternoon, I put out the automatic feeder and water bowl for Move-over, made sure his litter box was clean, and put the lights and radio on timers so anyone looking in would think someone was home. I got into my pickup and drove to Tabitha's college. It was already dark when I got there. She met me at the lounge next to the main entrance to her dorm.

I pulled her in and held her. The relief of seeing her okay was so great. I don't know how long we stood there in each others arms but everyone was staring by the time we moved apart.

"We need to talk. Private. Let's go up to my room."

She swung around. Using the single crutch she needed to walk and with her cast as a prod, she pushed through the students in the lobby to the elevators. She already had the doors closing on the elevator car when I got there.

"Slow poke."

"If I had a stick I could use for crowd control, I would have gotten here at the same time you did." We just held hands until we got inside her room. I wanted to hold her again but she pushed me away and told me about what she found out from Suzie. She insisted on me telling her everything I had done during the week before she let me pull her to the bed.

I was struggling with her bra straps before I thought to ask, "Where is your roommate?"

"She went home for the weekend."

We stopped talking for the rest of the night. I woke up in the morning to the metallic sound of claws on a window screen. It was something I was very familiar with, after all my family always had cats. I have expected a cat hanging from the window even if we were four stories up but it turned out to be a little nuthatch hanging upside down and watching.

"Ever since I got back to school, those birds have been hanging on that screen. I don't know why. There is no food out there and the trees are on the other side of the dorm."

"Tabby, I need to tell you the story that my Uncle Ben told be about Vietnam...

"I don't know how it fits but I somehow feel that we are now point men. Ever since the day those punks tried to take you, I have felt the danger building. Every day I feel myself become more attuned to what is around me. I wish I knew what those, those ... Yosie are thinking..."

Chapter 10
Testing

Spring was melting the snow. I wished I could be outside more but those pesky emails I sent to the colleges and labs had started a series of responses that took at least three hours every day to answer. The rebuilding of the Contraption was finished and I was starting measurements. I had hung a sixteen-pound bowling ball from the rafters and was measuring the strength of the gravity field by marking the deflection of the ball from the perpendicular. I learned my lesson from the first experiment and set the transmitter strengths to their lowest settings. The ball still moved more than a half a meter to the focus from a point one and a half meters away. I had set the ball closer but the gravity field had pulled the ball into the focus and it reflected the lasers causing the field to collapse.

I was counting the days to when Tabitha would be home during Easter break with both anticipation and worry. I wanted to show her the Contraption and bring her to see Uncle Ben if the weather held. But I also noticed that the numbers of watchers had increased. I was hoping that it was just because the warmer temperatures had brought more animals out and not that they were waiting for something to see.

***

The Chameleon had just organized the take-over of a

smaller publishing firm. She ripped the pieces of the company apart and fired most of the workers. It resulted in a net gain of two million dollars to the company. Most of the money came from the retirement accounts of the workers. The smaller company had banked most of the retirement accounts into its own coffers. With the company in pieces, the Chameleon had been able to liquidate the accounts and substitute the cheapest retirement plan she could find. This place was already boring her. It was just a pale imitation of the Users. The joy she felt when she first discovering the intricacies of this society had faded to contempt with the ease of her infiltration. She decided that she would collect all the information the Users needed in a few more months.

***

"Wow! Have you been busy. Okay, no coaching. Let's see if I can figure out everything you have done."

Tabitha spent the next hour looking over the changes I made to the Contraption. It was three times larger than when she left for school. Most of the size was accounted for with the inch and a quarter pipe that I used as a frame for mounting the transmitters.

"Okay, I understand the harness around the dish. I can see how you used the pipes to mount the transmitters. Did I ask why so large pipes? Wait, I seem to remember you saying something about having them already. I understand the bowling ball pendulum for measuring the gravitational strength. Could you tell me again why you have the transmitters mounted away from the dish?"

"Remember that gravitational strength decreases with the square of the distance?"

"Right, right. The extra distance lowers the force enough so the gravity doesn't affect the transmitters. I got everything but what the hell is that copper pipe and rubber hose for."

"Remember that all we got was a distortion when we first turned on the Contraption until Move-over dropped the dust bunny?"

"Yup."

"Well it took me a while to figure out what might have happened. I decided that the gravitational field was forming and the energy of the air molecules being accelerated around the forming field caused the distortion we saw. The combination of moving air and forming field caused the gravity field to fluctuate as well. A strong field couldn't form because everything was rippling until the concentrated mass of the dust bunny made contact with the energy. I was going to drop small pieces of dirt into the field to get things started but I realized that the lasers would bounce off the dust so I decided to minimize the bounce by injecting an air stream."

"Turn it on. I got to see this."

There was a humming and the boombox vibrated with the Mozart piece I put in the player. The distortion field formed and I blew into the rubber hose. Air streamed out the small copper tube and the field formed. A small blue ball of light glowed from where the focus of the dish was and a soft whistling sound came from the copper tube as air swirled around the blue ball. The bowling ball moved slowly to the focus. The blue ball faded and dissolved into a distortion field again. I blew into the hose and the gravitation ball formed once more.

"The field breaks down so I have to periodically blow a new concentrated air flow into the system. The blue glow I think comes from the near by air molecules collapsing in on themselves. I think..."

I never got a chance to finish. Tabitha jumped me. We wrestled in the garage for a while, hands sneaking between layers of clothing. Finally, I ran and she hopped with her half cast leg into the house and the warmth of the bedroom.

The spring floods had come. I could never figure out where my uncle went when his cabin was flooded out.

There was still snow on the north side of the trees and a nip to the air. Tabitha had helped pack the supplies and canoe into the pickup. It took an extra hour to pack but it was the most fun I had ever had loading-up.

Tabitha couldn't get comfortable with her cast sitting in the prow so I had her sit as cargo in the middle of the canoe. We were slowly drifting downstream. We floated past a bend and I saw the hollowed out woodpecker tree. The Pileated Woodpecker wasn't there but an eagle watched from the top of the tree.

I caught a whiff of wood smoke, the distinctive smell of cedar with the pungent mix of birch. I knew that Ben was near. Just past the next bend, Ben waved us to shore. The near bank was heavily flooded so we had to wade the supplies to Ben's canoe and ourselves to shore. Tabitha didn't want to get her cast wet and asked Ben for a lift. He was laughing so hard he nearly dropped her into the river. At the campfire, he had opened a can of coffee and started brewing. I don't know how he knew but he had three birch bark cups made and ready for us to drink from.

We drank the coffee slowly just making small talk about the early spring. Ben disappeared behind some trees and came back with a beautiful four-foot walking stick. It was made from twisted white ash and had been oiled to a bright sheen. Handing it to Tabitha, "This for you. Much better than crutches. Can I show you?"

Tabitha handed it back. Ben took it. Suddenly the stick was spinning, flying through the air. Ben did a series of smacks to a small tree, head height, stomach, and feet ending with the point of the stick smashing into the heart of the imaginary tree man. He handed the walking stick back.

"You have puukko?" I pulled the knife from where I hung in under my left arm. "Good. She will need a knife too. Take her today and buy her a good one."

Turning to Tabitha, "He told you about being at point. But remember being at point is more than just you and everything else. There are those following." He stopped talking and refilled our bark cups.

He carried Tabitha back to the canoe. Before he could back away, she grabbed him by his scraggly beard and kissed him. Ben fell on his ass, waist deep in the water. He started laughing, splashing water at Tabitha and me. "Dan you better take good care of her. I recommend a good spanking when you get home." Tabitha flushed to a bright red. But when she turned back to look at me her eyes had a bright sparkle.

The eagle watched us as we paddled upstream.

When we got into town, I bought Tabitha two knives. I couldn't find a puukko so I bought a Marine Kabar and a balanced throwing knife. We were very sober by the time we got back home until Tabitha dropped her pants and reminded me that I was suppose to give her a spanking.

It was May and the emails were becoming a real problem. Finally, I decided that the easiest thing to do was to schedule a demonstration. Tabitha said that she would be done with her classes by the twenty-eighth. I decided to give the demonstration on the thirtieth. After checking the date with Tabitha, I sent emails to everyone giving the date and location. I put in for two weeks vacation at the end of May and got back to proofreading.

***

The Chameleon was mad at herself. She had been so busy playing games with her new identity that she forgot to keep up with the scientific news. Her neglect was brought to her attention when she reviewed travel expenses for her company's science magazine. The physics reporter was asking for expenses to go to Northern Minnesota. When she questioned him, he showed her a dozen pages of equations and experiments that were being done all over the world. All of the work was based on an original set of equations from a Daniel Karpinen. Everyone was questioning if Karpinen actually did the original work. He was a proofreader for a competing publisher and not a known research scientist. The speculation had become a topic between all of the science/mathematics magazines and had increased the interest in Karpinen and his equations. Karpinen was set to run an experiment based on his equations for anyone interested on May 30th. After a quick check, the Chameleon found that most of the scientific publishing world and many of the scientific labs were sending people to Minnesota.

The Chameleon had to stop the demonstration. She was not an expert in physics but she was skilled enough to recognize a quantum leap in technology. Some aspects of gravitational control showed by the equations would put this *human* race at close to equal footing with the Users. She had to find out what Karpinen knew and who he told. She then had to destroy the work in such a way as to give the impression that the whole thing was a scam.

The first thing she did was tell her reporters to be very careful with the story. Reminding them of the cold fusion fiasco of a few years ago, she told them they had to be supercritical of the event. There was only a week and a half left before the demonstration. She had her staff detectives make an emergency physical review of Karpinen's home. While waiting for the report, she would travel north preparing for the sabotage.

May 27th. The Chameleon finally received the detective's reports. She was staying a half a day's drive from Karpinen's home. The farm looked isolated. The phone and power lines seemed easy to compromise.

***

Jones was nearly finished with Blythe. He had tried to stop the takeover of Blythe's companies but after the Coffee Klutch drew first blood, the Wall Street sharks chewed apart his companies. His last act for Blythe was to arrange some physical act against Karpinen. He had put it off until now knowing that the police would zero in on both him and

Blythe. His thoughts were interrupted by the conversation at the booth behind him.

"The motel is already full. I counted stringers from *Scientific American*, *Nature*, and *Popular Science*. I glanced over the check-in-counter at the motel and the last room was reserved for Professor Schmitt from Argon National Labs."

"I interviewed Professor Manning at JPL last week. I asked him about Karpinen. He didn't say anything... But you know Manning. He was interested."

"This is going to be the biggest scientific event of the decade and no one in the mainstream media has come out with it yet. Even if Karpinen is a fraud, there has to be something there. Otherwise, Manning, Schmitt, and all those others would be tearing him apart by now."

"I think that might be the reason the networks haven't broken the news yet. No one knows for sure yet so we are all holding our breaths until we know..."

Jones thought, "To-hell-with-Blythe." He paid his check, got into his car and drove away. Later that night, Blythe put a 9 millimeter Glock to the side of his head and pulled the trigger.

***

Tabitha came over at daybreak. Some juice and toast and we started setting up. I jacked the main body of the Contraption onto a dolly. We were rolling it to the corner of the yard so it would be easier for everyone to see it work.

A car pulled up and this slinky brunette slide out. "Hello. I am Jennifer Cosgrove from the Benton Publishing Group International."

"I am sorry but the demonstration is scheduled for the day after tomorrow."

"I am not here for the demonstration. I want to talk to you."

Suddenly, I noticed that the crows on the fence line were watching the woman. From the corner of my eye, I saw a quizzical look come on Tabitha's face. I watched the woman closely and started to notice things. "I am sorry but I really don't have time to talk now. We are setting up."

I took a few steps away from the Contraption. She moved as well to stay facing me. Her body swayed sexily but something was not right. It was as if her joints didn't bend the same as everyone else. In high school, I had a friend with severe arthritis. She didn't move the same as everyone else. This woman reminded me of her.

"It will only take a few minutes. We need a proofreader of your caliber at Benton."

"I am sorry but you will just have to come back after the demonstration." Faster than I would have thought possible, the woman took a gun out of her bag. I rolled to the ground. When I stopped, I threw the puukko. Before my knife hit, the woman stood with an astonished look on her face and gun dangling from her fingers. Tabitha's throwing knife was sticking out of her left chest. My knife took her in the throat.

***

The Chameleon struggled to live. The genetically engineered body could have handled one piece of metal penetrating her body but two were too much. She should have skipped regulations and brought a User weapon instead of this primitive planet's gun. This planet was just... The biomechanical chip inside the Chameleon's body registered the fact that her body had stopped functioning. A message was sent to the Chameleon's ship. The automatic destruction sequence started. A thousand message pods were sent expelled in random directions with the details of everything the Chameleon did and the ship plunged itself into the surface of the sun.

The message pods traveled until they sensed a ship belonging to the Users near. Out of the thousand pods twenty made it to User ships. The data was analyzed and sent to the regional control ship.

The Chameleon gone! What could have happened? This was a primitive planet. A sanitation squad needed to be sent. All links to the Users the Chameleon left had to be severed and revenge taken.

***

I looked at Tabitha. "How did you know?"

"She didn't look right. I don't know... Something about her didn't add up. I had my hand on the knife before she reached for the gun."

I looked back at the woman. Something was definitely wrong. The blood coming from the wounds was not the right shade of red. Her body seemed to be deflating. I reached down and touched her arm. It was too limp. I picked it up. The bones in the arm were deflating. "God, the woman's bones are not bones." I continued feeling the arm. "I think they are some kind of tough inflatable skin. An organ in the body must pump fluid in and the skin/bones become rigid and take form. Look at how the outer skin is loosing form. This creature ... this woman is a creature..."

"What are we going to do?"

"I don't know. No one will believe what has happened."

"We've got to hide the body."

"I'll check the car. You check the purse."

I found a piece of paper with the letterhead of a near by Holiday Inn. Tabitha found a door card key in the purse.

"Let's put her in the car and park it at the hotel. We will leave the body in the car and let the authorities try to figure everything out."

"Good. But we will need to not leave fingerprints."

I looked at the body. It had become a puddle of flesh on the ground. A brunette wig was lying next to where the head had once been. "Tabitha. Can you drive her car? If you put the wig on, people might think it was her behind the wheel."

We had trouble moving the creature's body into the car.

It was like trying to move a 40-gallon plastic bag half filled with water. You would get your hands under an edge and lift. All of the internal fluid would flow to the end of the bag and you would be lifting just the flexible outer layer. Every time we lifted a section away from the two knife wounds blood, or whatever it was, would gush from the openings. We finally oozed the creature into the passenger seat where she flowed to the floor.

The drive to the Holiday Inn parking lot was uneventful. Tabitha left the car at the far end of the lot and limped across the street to where I waited with the pickup. I drove to a payphone. Dialed 911. "There is something strange in the parking lot at the Holiday." I hung up and drove home without saying a thing.

Two hundred people showed up for the demonstration. We watched the crowd for anything unusual.

Chapter 11
Government

There are two types of government officials in Washington, the political appointees and professional bureaucrats. Thomas Riley was a professional. He started in the State Department five administrations ago. Over the years he had served in the Justice Department, the CIA and the NSA. When the last President was elected, he was in the Security Council. The President had tried to get a good politician in the job of National Security Advisor but his original candidate had a youthful discretion that was discovered by the tabloids. When the appointee was seventeen years old, he was picked up by the police with two other boys and three girls. The cops found open beer cans, two joints of marijuana, and three amphetamines in the car. With the original appointee out, the President had decided on using a safe but dumb politician for the job. With a political figurehead in the top position, a true National Security Advisor had to be found. As a result, Riley had become the de facto National Security Advisor and had not had a full night's sleep in the last two years.

The current problem was a nightmare. A month ago local police in rural Minnesota were called to a suspicious car. The local crime lab took one look at what had been found and called the FBI. The FBI forensic team's preliminary report went all the way to the President's desk. A team of scientists from NASA, Department of Defense, FBI, and a few well-vetted biology professors were assigned the job of analyzing the remains. The first interim report from the whole team had made it to Riley's desk this morning. The report stated without qualms that the remains were not terrestrial. The genetic code of the creature was not dependent on earth type chromosomes but a unique DNA/RNA mix of small molecular chains within a cell's nucleus. The creature's physical structure was even more extreme. The creature had been similar in structure to a squid or an octopus with skeleton rigidity coming from fluid inflatable bones. There was evidence of sutures tying muscles and bones together indicating that the creature was surgically constructed to have a similar appearance to humans.

Earlier that week a second team from the FBI and CIA had sent in an analysis of the circumstances around the timing and location of the alien remains. The only thing that made sense was that the creature had successfully took over the life of one, Jennifer Cosgrove, an executive with Benton Publishing. She, or it, was going to see the demonstration of gravitational control scheduled two days later at the Daniel Karpinen farm. Someone or something decided to kill the alien. Since the consensus of the FBI/CIA team was that Karpinen was important, it was recommended that everything that could be done to help Karpinen in his work should be done and that he should be protected.

For the last few hours, Riley was struggling on the wording of the sealed Executive orders that the President had asked him to write. Every time Riley started on the draft, he got lost with the idea of aliens actually being on earth. He kept expecting to wake up any minute in his old battered armchair with *X-files* and *Outer Limits* reruns playing on the TV. Damn, he wished he knew how to write these things but the President had ordered him not to contact anyone about the orders. After printing out the orders, the proscribed procedure was to use a scrubbing utility on the computer to eliminate any information still on the hard drive. Damn secrecy, how was he suppose to make sure his wording was legal? Finally after hours of work, the drafts were ready.

By order of the President of the United States the following procedures are to be immediately implemented:

The National Security Council will coordinate and develop new screening methods to protect all strategic sites from infiltration by non-humans.

The Department of Defense will develop new surveillance procedures and weapons to protect the earth from intrusion from non-terrestrial sources.

Updates of the new security arrangements will be given to the Select Committee of Congress and the President monthly through the National Security Council.

The cover story of "an increased threat by terrorist groups with access to missile/biological technology" will be given to any questions about the changes in security, funding priorities, and Defense changes. Information not cleared for public dissemination through the Select Committee and the President will be considered high treason.

_____
President of the United States

_____
Date

By order of the President of the United States the FBI, CIA, and the Department of Defense will set up a surveillance of the Daniel Karpinen and his farm. Karpinen will not be interfered with but observed and protected. All recordings and information collected will be sent by courier to the Security Council for analysis. Summaries of the information will be given directly to the President every month.

The Department of Defense and NASA will fund and place an office within the Security Council that will process the information gathered and supply money and help for Daniel Karpinen's work. This help must be screened so no one outside the Security Council will know that it is being done.

Information not cleared for public dissemination by the President will be considered high treason.

_____
President of the United States

_____
Date

***

Felix Abercrombie drove up to the farm. Before he could get to the door, an agent got out and told him to park the car in the large equipment shed. Inside, Felix saw two large SUVs and three other tan sedans. When he got back to the house, he was told he was late and to go into the living room where the briefing was about to start. There were no empty chairs left so he stood by the back wall. A man stood up.

"My name is Harry Zimmerman. I will be in charge of this operation. You should have been informed by now that this will be a long-term undercover operation. Because of the rural nature of the location, you will be rotated out to a Twin Cities hotel for one week off every month. While here, you will be required to keep out of sight and work cover chores on the farm. The location is unique plus we don't want the target to know we are here so we will be depending mostly on remote sensors and field intelligence through local law enforcement. The locals do not know about us but have been given a heads-up about the target and their frequencies are being monitored for pertinent information.

"Our target is living on a farm three quarters of a mile away. You are to observe and protect the target. We have taps on the phone lines into the farm but we have yet to place surveillance equipment in the house. One of the first duties we have will be to insert listening devices and recorders on the target's property.

"This is a joint project and I will not tolerate any inter-agency rivalries. I expect you to follow your orders and work as a team.

"Our military liaison is Major Stanley Burrows. Major, please stand and introduce yourself. And tell the staff what your duties will be."

"I am Major Burrows. I will coordinate all information from the Pentagon. I will be commanding all military personnel at this site. I am also authorized to call in either a Delta team or a rapid-deployment company stationed at Fort Ripley."

"Next is John Smith coordinating with the CIA."

"Hello. My name is really John Smith so no jokes. I will have access to background information and analysis for all non-US contacts that the target makes. If you need information outside FBI channels, come to me."

"I am leading the FBI team here as well so I will make the introductions for the rest of the FBI personal. Jeremiah Francisco grew up only a hundred miles from here. He will be acting as the owner of the farm and will be the major contact with the locals.

"Stand up Jeremiah."

"The three man close-up team has worked together for the last year. Todd Rittmiller specializes in electronics. Sam Aizawa is cross training. And Felix Abercrombie is long range surveillance and sniper.

"Okay, guys stand up.

"The close up team will immediately start reconnaissance of the target farm and work on placement of surveillance equipment. The rest of us will start working on support procedures. The remotes will be recorded and analyzed off-site. There are duplicate receivers and recorders in the communication room at the head of the stairs. I expect everyone to spend time in the room familiarizing yourselves with the target and other civilians who might be at the site. You will be expected to distinguish the good guys from the bad. If headquarters determines that intervention is need, this red light/siren will come on with details broadcast in the communication room."

Felix took the lead. He was the best in the woods. The team had spent an hour going over aerial photographs and topographical maps of the area around the target's farm. Felix immediately went into stalking mode. Todd's and Sam's stumbling and noise pushing through the brush were an annoyance. He was having trouble scanning the near by woods. "Be quiet. The information we have is that the target goes into the woods frequently." There was a snort in reply but the noise lessened.

They just waded through a muddy low spot when Felix felt eyes watching his every move. He raised his hand to stop the rest of the team and tried to find the source of his uneasiness. He found nothing but the sense of being watched finally quieted the rest of the team and in silence they made it to the edge of the field surrounding the target's farm. The team settled down to watch the farm trying to recognize any patterns that they could use to get close enough to plant their surveillance devices. Felix used a parabolic mike and his riflescope to examine the farm buildings while Sam used binoculars and Todd a specially designed long-range video camera.

There was a lot of activity at the farm. Five people were going in and out of a metal building. There were sounds of metal-working and a boombox playing rock. It was midmorning when the target Daniel Karpinen and his girl friend Tabitha Czeminski came out of the main house. They were halfway to the metal building when they stopped and looked right at the team. Their conversation had been muffled by the wind until they turned. Felix froze hearing, "Two or three?"

"Three."

"What do you think?"

"Harmless so far but we will have to keep an eye out for them."

"Right."

They turned and continued to the building.

Felix hissed, "What the hell happened. How did they know?"

"What are you talking about?"

"They knew we were here. I picked them up talking about us on the mike."

"God."

"Todd. Sam. Check and see if we tripped any sensors. I will keep an eye on the farm." It was fifteen minutes later when the others reported that there was nothing. The team moved to the other side of the field carefully searching the area for sensors or other watchers. Settling in the new location, Felix had Sam keep an eye at the surrounding woods while Todd and he watched the farm.

It was late in the day and the five other people at the farm had gotten into cars and driven away. Karpinen and his girlfriend paused to look at their new location before going into the farmhouse.

Sam, anxious to get the job done, "Should we go close and plant the bugs?"

"No, they know we are here. I don't know how they know but they know. We're leaving for now.

"The woods are going to be hard going in the dark. I will take point. Watch my steps."

They were crossing the marsh again. Todd and Sam had become stuck in the mud and were splashing when a voice came out of the darkness. "You will have to do better than that if you are going to help my nephew. You need to step back and just follow their point." The team pulled their weapons and donned their night vision goggles but found nothing.

When Felix reported in to Zimmerman, he recommended that they have one of the people working at the farm plant the bugs. Zimmerman told him that one of the workers at the farm was an agent but that they hadn't been able to get a bug operational in the house just in the metal building. Felix's team had to control access to the farm from the woods and try to get a device into the farmhouse. Felix agreed to try again at three in the morning to plant devices at the house.

The team was dropped off near the farm from the road. They crept up to the house. Tonight they would try to place button microphones on a few of the windows. Felix was just placing the mike. He glanced into the home and nearly screamed. A cat had its face up against the window watching. They finished planting the mikes and rushed back to the base.

Felix, Todd and Sam sat together in the communications room while Todd fiddled with the gain on the microphones. There were five monitors recording the night sounds at the farm -- bedroom, computer room, kitchen, dining room, and living room. They hardly had an hour of tape before they heard a heavy rumbling and a crunch. The bedroom mike stopped. "The god-damn cat must have ate the mike. That rumbling had to be a cat's purr." By eight o'clock, all the microphones were dead. Todd screamed and pulled the headphones he was using off when the kitchen mike was destroyed. Todd had increased the gain on the last microphone to maximum trying to catch the sounds of Karpinen waking up in the back of the house when a chickadee announced its presence at the window followed by the silence of a broken mike.

Chapter 12
Submarine

I am usually a little maudlin in the mornings eating breakfast. I couldn't believe what happened over the last few months since we were forced to kill that creature. The demonstration of the Contraption went too well. Everyone wanted more. Even my company told me to take a leave of absence and work on converting electromagnetic energy into gravity. Requests for information and offers of help and grants poured in.

It was two weeks after the demonstration and Tabitha had finally had her cast removed. We were parked in my pickup next to the video store. "Tabby, what should I do?"

"If you think you can handle the scrutiny of everyone looking over your shoulder at what you are doing, you should go for it. They are offering you anything you need. Why not see what will happen? No matter what happens, you still have shaken the scientific world."

"Tabby."

"Yes."

"Could you handle staying with me through all of this?"

She leaned into me laying her head on my shoulder. "Yes."

Tap. Tap. Tap. "Kids, not in front of the store. You will drive away customers." Earl was smiling through the window he had just rapped.

We drove back to my home. I printed the research offers and spread them across the living room floor. Move-over immediately started to swat at the paper. The offers to work theoretical mathematics were the first to be wadded into balls and rolled to Move-over for attack. The energy and particle proposals were the next to go to the cat. We were finally left with two. The first was from the University of Minnesota and NASA. The U of M would supply graduate students and technical support for exploring the use of artificial gravity in space/transportation. The list of questions that they wanted answers to ranged from artificial gravity in spacecraft to the feasibility of using gravity in high speed trains. NASA would also supply monetary and technical help to the project. The second was from the Jet Propulsion Lab. They were offering an actual position at the lab to work on artificial gravity to counter the affects of low gravity on the physiology of astronauts.

"Dan. Take the U of M and NASA. We could work here."

"Okay. Give me the phone number off the proposal and I will call them."

Tabby smiled and stuck the paper down her blouse. "Why don't you just come and get it."

I shook my head. Tabby and I had so little time to play since then. The half a dozen grad students were always around during the day. The original Contraption was relegated to the corner of the garage. Nearly immediately we received a tungsten steel sphere for the new experiments. The sphere made it possible to completely control what was occurring with the EM, electromagnetic, conversion to gravity but it also meant we needed an industrial drill press, diamond drill bits, and other industrial grade equipment. We received new transmitters from NASA specially made to withstand high stress forces. They had been originally designed for shuttle/satellite use. The first time we tried out the sphere we found two things. The gravity being produced was a hundred times stronger than with the original contraption and that the air being injected into the sphere to start the reaction was super heated and could blow out any weak point in the sphere. A transducer was blown through the wall of the garage and into the side of one of the grad student's car fender. We decided to move the sphere to the metal shed, which was farther from the house.

The next thing to happen with the new sphere came straight out of a Road Runner and Coyote cartoon. Just after the whistling of the exhaust vent started, things started to fly into the sphere as the gravity became great enough to pull small items that were lying higher than the sphere. The cartoon type attraction got me scared. I decided to stop experimenting until I could check out the possibility that we might create a singularity or mini black hole in the shed. A few weeks later, Argon laboratories verified that we couldn't mistakenly destroy the world so we got back to playing with different frequencies and combinations trying to calibrate the combinations of electromagnetic energy that could be converted to gravity.

We couldn't decide what to do next after the calibrations until we got a dozen baseball size spheres from the Jet Propulsion Labs. The people at JPL noticed that everything we had been using was already miniaturized for commercial use somewhere in the world. There were LED lasers for fiber optics and even color displays. Micro-transmitters of all kinds were built for everything from toys to watches. They decided to make small enough spheres that you could place them under the floor or bulkhead on the Space Station. You could have a room with a whole floor layered with artificial gravity devices. The first time I heard the dozen different notes from the exhaust ports on the miniature spheres I remembered how everything seemed to start after seeing those birds. And that got me thinking about flight.

Tabby refused to stay nights with me. She would come early in the morning leaving late in the evening. I wanted her with me all the time but she insisted on staying at her home for now. I could hear the grad students starting to arrive and knew she would be coming through the front door soon.

She blew in with a smile on her face. I could tell she had gone for a morning run. She always looked excited after running and the full natural musk of exercise filled the air around her. "Hi, Move-over. Been giving your master trouble?"

"Meerrroow."

"Good boy." Turning to me, "Have you been a good boy while I've been gone?"

"No. What are you going to do about it?"

She dived in close. Bit my ear. Grabbing my crotch, she whispered, "Good, I like bad little boys."

"I love you."

She stopped. Her face suddenly serious. "I know." She smiled and was again her playful self. "But you are going to have to suffer a little more before I will let you do anything about it."

The mood was broken. "I've got an idea about handling the venting of the air from the large sphere."

"Great. What?"

"I am thinking about asking NASA for a movable control jet. If we attach the sphere to a plane we could pull the plane forward and use the movable jet to control the motion. Of course, nothing would work with just the large sphere. But if you put the small spheres in the wings and trigger them in sequence we could get airflow and lift."

"Wait a sec... Would an airframe hold up to the stress..."

We left the house an hour later with more instructions for the grad students. I felt eyes. Intelligent eyes. We looked to the edge of the woods. I didn't feel the uneasiness of danger so we went back to work.

The next morning Tabby found me in my workroom. I was sending email and talking on the phone. "Here you are. Do you think you could use a hand?" Tabby looked over the pile of post-it-notes and printouts.

"Bye now, I'll talk to you later." I pressed the off switch on the headset. "Tabby, could you hang up the phone?"

"Sure. What's the rush?"

"I think I have found an answer to the stress problem on the airframe. I found a submarine."

"What?"

"The U of M Limnology Department wanted a small submarine to study Lake Superior and a few other lakes in the state. They didn't have the money for purchasing one so the engineering school started to make one. They got the main structure built and the power plant installed when an alumnus donated a submarine to the school. The sub was never finished. I am just finishing arrangements to have it sent up."

"Well a submarine would be strong enough for the gravitational forces but it sure will be ungainly looking. What are you thinking of using for the wings."

"I decided to call the Air Guard base in Duluth. For some reason, the Colonel in charge talked to me. Well, I found out a C130 Hercules caught fire and burned in Grand Forks a few months back. The elevators of the plane should work for our test so I got NASA to take possession of the elevators. They should be here about the same time as the submarine."

"A submarine with left over cargo plane parts? It can't be safe."

"We can start by checking the lift on the ground."

I finished sending the last email and submarined under Tabby's shirt.

***

Felix was frustrated. Zimmerman was pushing hard to get onsite surveillance but everything they tried failed. It was like the animals were helping Karpinen. When he tried to explain about the cat and the birds wrecking the bugs, Zimmerman said nonsense. Karpinen had to be feeding the animals near his house and that was why they destroyed the bugs. When Felix got back to his team, he overheard Sam telling Todd something about Yosei.

"What's Yosei?"

"You don't want to know."

"Tell."

"My grandmother would tell me bedtime stories. She had a few favorites about Yosei. Yosei are sort-a-like fairies but not. Birds can be Yosei. My grandmother would say that Yosei are protecting Karpinen and that we better respect them or we will be in trouble."

"Well there are no Yosei. I am more worried about who talked to us the first night we were out. Harry finally let lose with some information. It turns out the Karpinen has an uncle. He served two tours in Nam. I saw some of his records. He specialized at point on recon teams. That must have been him out there. We need to watch out for him. He is one mean mother. He took out fifteen VC when his camp was over-run during something called the Quang Tri Offensive. The last five he used his knife on."

***

Ole Swenson started with Lockhead Martin ten years ago. His transfer to Palmdale and the Skunk Works had been a goal since his first model airplane, a SR-71. When he got to the Skunk Works, it was a disappointment. There were no secret projects or impossible deadlines. That was until a few weeks ago.

It all started with a phone call telling him to fly to Washington. When he arrived at NASA headquarters he was discretely taken out the backdoor and driven to an underground garage. A walk down a long hall followed by an elevator ride and he arrived at the office of Thomas Riley the Assistant National Security Advisor. Since then, Ole's life had become a living hell of impossible schedules coordinating the tasks of dozens of scientists and engineers while at the same time trying to placate the military and business bureaucrats who thought he was usurping their jobs. He loved it.

The intercom buzzed. "Sir. Your call to Dryden Flight Center is on line 3. The report from JPL just came in and when you have time you can check the letter I typed to Sanders. If you could finish it before 2 o'clock I can get it on the company shuttle to Nashua."

"Thank you, Nancy." The smile on Ole's face broadened. He could kiss Daniel Karpinen for making his aeronautic dreams come true.

"Hello Sam. Ole here. What did you find out about the airfoil design? Huh ... huh..."

Chapter 13
YS1

I could feel the crisp bite in the air of fall. The days and weeks of working with computers, grad students and power tools had taken their toll. I needed to go for a walk in the woods before the big event tomorrow. I grabbed Tabby when she came in and we crossed the frosted field to the trees.

The woods were silent after the power drills and grinders but only for a few seconds. The sounds of birds made themselves first known, followed by the wind and the rustling of the small creatures in the fallen leaves. I eased my feet between the dry leaves. The soft swoosh of Tabby's steps followed me deeper into the woods. Occasionally, I would point out a bird or animal that was seldom seen, a great gray owl, rose-breasted grosbeak, a lynx...

We twisted back and forth through the woods watching and breathing the fresh air. A noise softer than the rustle of a mouse through the leaves but louder than the steps of a deer drifted from ahead. The small birds near by started glancing towards the new sounds. I signaled Tabby and we hid behind a deadfall. A few minutes later three men dressed in camouflage, armed, and packing cameras and sound equipment walked past. Just after they left, "I think they are FBI but they might be military."

"Ben. What are you doing here?"

"Keeping an eye on you. Those men have been watching you for months."

"I know."

"Good boy. You are learning."

"Let's find out how good these guys are. Why don't you bring me my supplies next week?"

"Okay. But if you have been staying near wouldn't it be easier if I just canoe down the river here."

"I don't want them to know how close I am.

"Be careful. I feel trouble coming."

Before Ben could leave, Tabby gave him a kiss. Giggling, he picked up his rifle and disappeared into the woods. That scared me. I seldom saw Ben carrying a rifle.

"Something is very bad if Ben is carrying the 30-30."

"It doesn't look in good shape. Do you think we should buy him a new rifle?"

"My father gave him that Winchester carbine when he stopped hunting about ten years ago. Ben loves the rifle because it is from dad. I've seen him bark a squirrel at 150 feet with it."

"Bark a squirrel?"

"You hit a squirrel with a 30-30 and there is nothing left of it to eat so you shoot next to the squirrel. The bark and splinters from the tree getting hit will kill the squirrel."

"Remind me to ask what's for dinner before I accept any food from him."

"You should-n-of-said that. Now we will have something different to eat the next time we see him." From Tabby's smile, I knew she expected that. She was just teasing Ben and me.

Tabby turned serious. "How did you know those men were coming?"

"Small animals have to go through fall leaves so they are noisy. Deer, bear, wolves ... all large animals lift their feet above the leaves so they are quieter than the small animals. Those men were making less noise than a squirrel or a mouse but more than a deer. The sound was also without a simple rhythm so it had to be coming from more than one source. Large animals seldom travel in tight groups that left men as the source of the sound."

"I've got to remember that."

We made it back to the farm without anything else strange happening. We stopped at the shed to see the Yellow Submarine. The submarine was a long cigar shape with thick glass portholes and a hatch attached to the top. There was a beach ball size lump just above the midline on both the nose and tail of the cigar. Each lump had swiveling nozzles on their top and bottom. The C130 Hercules elevators were massive stubby wings that barely fit on the cigar. Everything was painted the yellow/green florescent color that you find on some fire engines. On the side was painted in red outline the words 'Yellow Submarine' and near the back were the call letters YS1.

YS1 looked like it couldn't move on the three stubby wheels that we had welded to the bottom -- let alone fly. But the ground tests had the monstrosity lifting off the ground within a hundred yards. To play it safe, Tabby called the airplane manufacturer in Duluth to design and install a parachute for YS1.

It took hours of explanation before the NASA test pilot sent up from Edwards Airbase would even get into YS1. We had to show him the gravity balls inside the wings and the computer software that would turn the gravity on in sequence pulling air over the wings. After the first flight, we had trouble keeping the pilot out of YS1.

Since the Yellow Submarine didn't need air to fly, we were going to try a near space entry tomorrow. In the upper atmosphere, the gravity balls in the wings were turned off and the power was fed into the large ball in front pulling YS1 higher and higher. The result was YS1 slowly going to ever greater altitudes. At first, no one believed the sedate speed YS1 used as it climbed. After I sent the first flight reports to the U of M and NASA, I had a dozen officials asking to view the next test.

The big event started before dawn with lawn chairs set out by the metal shed. A Dr. Scott from the Marshall Space

Flight Center in Huntsville arrived at five o'clock with a general from Edwards Air Force Base by the name of Holcum. General Holcum's mouth fell open when he saw the pilot and the technician climb into the Yellow Submarine wearing space suits. The general's mouth dropped even farther when he saw the sedate speed YS1 used crossing the open farm field before it became airborne.

The general walked up to our lawn chairs. "How long will the test last?"

"Dr. Scott was given a complete break down of today's testing. But you might as well relax. It will be awhile. YS1 will start climbing in large circles around the farm. The battery life on board is about twelve hours so the pilot will climb for five hours before coming back down. This will give us a two-hour cushion if a problem occurs and the pilot has to land at a different field." I backed away from the general and got out an old book of my father's that I found in a box in the attic. Louis L'Amour's *The Lonesome Gods* kept me company for most of the morning. Tabitha sat next to me reading a Cornwell murder mystery. After an hour, both the Dr. Scott and General Holcum grabbed a couple of lawn chairs and moved next to the radio where they could hear the pilot calling out speed and altitude numbers.

I looked at my watch. 10:59, nearly 5 hours after the six o'clock take off. I walked over to the radio. "What is the altitude?"

"He just radioed an altitude of 755,103 feet with a speed of 237 miles per hour."

"Let's see ... divide by 5,280 feet in a mile. My calculator tells me that is about 143 miles. Is that right?"

"Yes, 143 is what I make it."

"Call him up and tell him to head back down."

"YS1. YS1. This is base calling. Time to turn around and come home."

"Base. This is YS1. Roger. Heading home."

I headed back to my lawn chair and the *Lonesome Gods*. Behind me, I could hear the general stuttering to Dr. Scott.

"He just went back to his book. They made it into space and all he does is reads a western. My God doesn't he know what this means..."

***

Thomas Riley called the meeting to order. There were fifteen experts ranging from psychologists to physicists. Chairing the group was Dr. Schmitt form Argon National Labs and co-chairing was Dr. Manning from JPL.

"I have read over your summary. It tells me that Daniel Karpinen is a fairly intelligent individual with slightly above average skills in physics and mathematics. He is a stable personality with a very strong individualistic streak. But this doesn't tell me why an alien creature would try to contact him or how he is able to continually make new discoveries."

Schmitt felt it was his place to answer. "After looking over Karpinen's work, we found that his ideas were not beyond the possibilities of any reasonably skilled scientist or engineer except for his first discovery of EM conversion to gravity. That first discovery was a unique step that took an unusual intellect to find."

He looked to Dr. Jorge, the lead psychologist, and received a nod of agreement before continuing. "Science and engineering are as much an art as painting, music, or prose. You can have people very skilled in the technical aspects of science who can never develop a unique thought. But another individual, with limited training, can see a pattern in equations the same way a musician can see a pattern in notes. Karpinen's work as a proofreader has brought him the details of most of the different branches of science. He has been able to see, using his knack for patterns, how the sciences relate. Our best explanation is that he is an artist in science and he is such a unique artist that even beings outside of our solar system have recognized his talent."

"Okay. I guess I will have to accept that. No one else

has given me a better idea. But how about bringing him in to work directly with us?"

Dr. Jorge took over. "We have done as much testing and analysis that we can without actually working with the subject but we are in agreement. Even if you were able to convince Karpinen to work for the government, the simple fact that he was hired in a government job would stifle his creativity. We have even gone a step further and analyzed how his works affect on the scientific community as a whole. Using the super computers at JPL, we ran a chaotic system analysis of the scientific community's work since Karpinen's first announcement. Working independent of the formal scientific community's environment, Karpinen has exponentially accelerated the advancements of the community as a whole.

"In layman's terms, he does more for everyone as long as he stays doing what he is doing now."

"Damn. Is there any way your data could be wrong?"

"Nothing is one hundred percent certain but I am willing to bet my doctorate that we need to give Karpinen as much independence as possible."

Riley didn't enjoy the arguments with the other bureaucrats but he would ask for an increase in funding to protect and keep supporting Karpinen's work. Bureaucrats were the same everywhere. They wanted control. Riley had to convince everyone that as little control as possible was the only course that they could take.

Chapter 14
Revenge

Ship Captain Ree and Mission Commander Zblot planned.

"The Regional Command has limited our response to just your ship but this mission worries me. I want as much equipment and personnel that I can get."

"With the remotes that you want to bring, I can only supply one landing vessel and one high cover protector. We have the standard crew of six for the main ship and the four needed on the landing and protector vessels that leaves room for only nine more individuals. With a five man assault team, science specialist, xenobiologist, and yourself, you are left with just one more individual."

"I know. I know. More equipment or another specialist..."

Assault leader Ed hated the two infiltrators in his squad. He was always queasy working with individuals who would disappear in the infirmary for a day or two and comeback looking completely different. The infiltrators new four-limb arrangement of this planet was unusual but not overly. Most creatures had pairs of appendages. Four was the basic starting pair of limbs. But what was strange was the use of only two for movement and two for manipulation. The limbs just made Ed queasy. Maybe it was his love of his own six multi-use limb arrangement or maybe it was the knowledge that the legendary Chameleon had been killed on this planet, but Ed was worried and drove his team endlessly through assault exercises and technical details of the planet they were to land on.

Grup, the heavy weapons specialist was easily the most intelligent member of the team. Ed could tell he was worried about the assignment as well. Grup spent all of his wake cycles reading up on the planet or cleaning the weapons that would be taken planet side. The sound of Grup's six strong limbs taking apart and putting together the team's blasters and needlers gave the quarters the only familiar sound. Commander Zblot had started playing during all wake cycles video and sound recordings from the strange planet they were heading for. The team had been on enough planetary landings to know that recordings seldom had anything to do with the reality they would find but the videos seemed to have an inordinately large number of killing and maiming between members of the dominate species. This did not bode well for the success of the mission.

Trreee, the team clown, came in complaining about the lack of information about wind conditions on the planet. Trreee's wings would normally be in continual motion but they now barely fluttered. If he was nervous, the team was in trouble. Maybe if Ed talked to Commander Zblot, they could replace the planet videos with *Fleetec Lives* or the finals of the inter-quadrant disk ball matches.

Uubee was glad that Commander Zblot had included a second science specialist to the team. From the Chameleon's last communique, they knew that the inhabitants of planet H14-D102, or earthlings, had discovered a way to control gravity. Currently star travel was accomplished by using the gravity and energy fields near stars to form small tears in the fabric of space. This meant that space travel required heavily armored and expensive ships traveling from a near obit of one star to a near orbit of another. A solar system could easily be blocked from access just by surrounding their star with a few weapons platforms. The Users needed this new technology. Unfortunately for them, all they had from the

Chameleon was the formula that the earthlings had discovered, the fact that earth used a base ten numbering system, and the cultural recordings needed for the next infiltrator to use to blend in with the locals.

The number problem was fairly easy. Being a scientist, required the ability to translate numbers from any known base to the ideal base eighteen, six limbs three fingers per limb. But the equations were a different matter. They were filled with symbols that were not numbers. It was easy to discover that '=' meant that the information matched and that '+','-', 'x', and '÷' were simple operations on the numbers but what in *The Hell of the Lost of Debon* were 'α', 'β', 'λ', 'π', 'Σ'... And were letters sometimes used for what appeared to be variable names and at other times used for something else?

No physical artifacts from H14-D102 made it back. And the recordings showed little of the internal workings of the technology and science on the planet. The video used to transmit information around the planet was not compatible with the standard recorders so the Chameleon just recorded the transmitted pictures. If only, the Chameleon had taken apart a few devices and recorded what was inside. They had sorted through recording after recording trying to find enough matches between the local science and real science. *Debon*! The earthling science didn't even use a consistent grouping like the ideal three.

The klaxon sounded. Time to seal up for the dimensional jump to the next star. Only three more shifts to planet H14-D102. Maybe, he could talk Commander Zblot into staying hidden on the near by planetary satellite until they were able to fully translate the equations. But Zblot had made it clear early on that she would only permit data collection during the time it took to eliminate any evidence of the Chameleon's stay and to serve revenge on those who killed the famed infiltrator. The Users code for self-preservation required revenge for killing one of their own. The code was important. The Users had outlasted hundreds of other interstellar civilizations by following it.

It was just possible that Zblot would finish the cycle change between female and male before the mission started. Civilized people were always more agreeable after the standard seven year gender change. If Uubee timed the next request for observation to just before the last planet jump, maybe Commander Zblot might be finished with the sex transformation and put science before revenge. Uubee hoped so, because until they got a key to translating the equations he suspected that artificial gravity would stay with the inhabitants of H14-D102.

***

We had told everyone that they would be on their own for the day so it was no surprise when the dark full-size SUV followed us from the farm. Since I didn't see a canoe on the vehicle, I assumed they would try to follow with an inflatable. Pulling into the landing, I pulled the stern of the canoe out of the pickup box and Tabby grabbed the prow when it came to the end of the tailgate.

"Listen carefully. Since they didn't come to the landing, they are going to have to go through the woods to the river. Everything near by but this campground is scrub second growth woods. It will be a bitch just walking through let alone carry anything."

Tabby swung the prow into the water. "They must be getting better. I can't hear anything." Just then a small flock of ducks took off from the river one bend upstream.

I dropped the stern in and tied a line from the gunnel to a near by tree. "I guess they made it to the river's edge." We finished loading the canoe, untied and paddled downstream. We could hear an occasional splash of water coming from behind. When we got to the woodpecker tree, I was not surprised to see Ben in his old canoe floating in a backwater eddy. We drifted down behind him and followed him to the inlet of his small floating bog. I don't know how he did it but the mouth of the stream that Ben's cabin was on was now hidden with a small island of floating marsh grass. We slipped behind the island and waited.

The same three-man team we had seen before appeared on the river in a dark green inflatable raft. They were not paddling but were using a small electric motor. Ten minutes after they passed, we paddled up stream to Ben's cabin and unloaded his supplies.

Tabby's first comment about the cabin was, "How cozy."

Fighting back laughter, "It is, isn't it." I couldn't tell what was cooking in the pot because Ben had it covered. But whatever it was it smelled great. This time Tabby got the coffee cup while Ben and I drank ours out of soup cans.

Ben announced, "Lunch is ready. We can have more coffee when we finish eating."

I don't know where Ben pulled the carved wooden bowls from but before we had a chance to speak he pulled something from the pot and gave a bowl full to each of us. It looked like a stew of some kind. Dark white, green, and brown lumps were sitting in a thick gravy.

"Do you have spoons?"

"Just use your knives to poke the chunks out and you can drink the broth from the bowl. Bon appetite."

I started laughing so hard my sides hurt. I stabbed a chunk of meat with my puukko and plopped it in my mouth. It melted with savory richness. There were at least three different kinds of meat in the stew and four vegetables. The only items in the stew I think I recognized were a mushroom and a cattail root. All three of us ended the meal by slurping up the remaining dredges of the stew from the side of our bowls.

It was time to head back. We had let the surveillance team spend about three hours looking for us on the river. I got up and on cue we all went back to the canoes. Laughing Tabby said, "Great meal Uncle Ben. I will make the next one." She then planted a big wet kiss on Ben and climbed into the canoe.

We paddled back to the hidden stream mouth with Ben following in his canoe. We waited behind the floating island for an hour, until we heard splashing from down stream. The rubber raft soon appeared with the three men awkwardly trying to paddle it against the current.

After waiting for ten minutes, we said goodbye to Ben and paddled up stream ourselves. We soon caught up to the raft.

I had to rub it in. "Nice day? Isn't it great being out on the water on a beautiful fall day like today?"

"Oh... Hi. Ya. It is a nice day."

"Been fishing?"

"No, just ... ah ... checking out the river ... ah ... for ... ah ... hunting?"

"Okay, see you."

We soon got to the landing and pulled the canoe from the water. We had no trouble turning our backs on the men because we knew Ben would be watching. The raft just made it to the landing by the time we were finished.

***

Felix confronted Zimmerman. "Harry, it isn't working. Karpinen knows we are watching. He is playing with us."

"Orders are to observe from a distance and not to contact. You have to do better."

"How? His uncle is helping him. You've read his file. He is just about the best there is in the woods. We can't get close without them knowing."

"Orders. Just follow orders."

Felix left for his team. Todd and Sam were waiting. "Harry wouldn't budge."

"Damn. Well at least we get a lot of fresh air," said Sam.

"The fresh air I don't mind. It is when it comes with rain that I have a problem," replied Todd.

Felix broke in, "Why did you have to remind me that

the forecast for tomorrow is for rain?"

Wet and miserable the day of watching the house came to a close as the grad students piled into their cars and left. Felix stood, brushing the branch he had been sitting under. Water spilled off the remaining leaves and dribbled between his neck and collar. As the cold water sent wet chills down his back, Felix repeated, "Damn, damn, damn, damn."

Stamping his cold numb feet, Felix said, "That's it." He headed across the open field to the house. Todd and Sam followed only in a slightly better mood. When he got to the front door of the house, he knocked. The door opened.

"Finally decided to introduce yourselves."

"Look, Mr. Karpinen. You know we are here and we know you know. Can't we work something out?"

"Want to come in?"

"Can't. I 'm already disobeying orders by talking to you. If I come inside and my boss finds out, I will be gone."

"Okay. How about you spread a tarp and set up a small camp just inside of the tree line? That will make things a little more comfortable."

"Thanks. That will help."

After the men left, I snuggled into the living room couch with Tabby. "I think it is time I called someone about those men watching us. Do you have any ideas on who to contact?"

"Ben was pretty sure they were FBI. Why don't you just call them? But can't you do that tomorrow?" Tabby slipped her hand between the buttons on my shit. Little chills went up and down my body.

"Tomorrow will be soon enough."

***

Riley got the transcribed phone conversation that the FBI director had with Karpinen the next day. He reviewed the analysis of Karpinen from the select committee and decided that it was time to make limited contact. He buzzed his secretary. "Get me Daniel Karpinen on the phone."

"Hello. Mr. Karpinen."

"Yes."

"This is Thomas Riley from the National Security Council. We have been observing you for the last few months because we have information that assets outside of the United States might have an interest in you and your work.

"I am sorry if this has inconvenienced you and I hope you will cooperate with our continued observation. We will be as discrete as possible."

"Look Mr. Riley, I can't stop you from watching but before you get cooperation you will have to give me more information."

"I am sorry Daniel but I can not give you any more information."

"It is Mr. Karpinen until or if you are straight enough with me to prove I can trust you Thomas."

"Mind if I get back to you a little later?"

"Take your time. Maybe you should come out here so we can meet face to face."

"I will think about it. Goodbye Mr. Karpinen."

"Goodbye Mr. Riley."

"Tabby. That was a Mr. Riley from the National Security Council. I think it is time to take a break from our gravity work and take a look at what is going on around us."

"Makes sense. Why don't I go to the shed and use the workstation there to start poking around and you use your computer to find out about this Riley? We can meet back here for supper. I will send the grad students home for the next few days."

"Good idea. We are nearly done with the YS1 testing. We can give them a week off. Tell them we are exploring a new subject for the next project."

After Tabby left, I decided I needed some concentration music. I placed in the CD player Mozart's *Symphony 29* followed by Handel's *Water Music* and Bach. To pull me out from the computer I decided to go with some female hard rock, Scandal, Pat Benatar, and Joan Jett.

By the end of Mozart, I knew that Thomas Riley was the real National Security Advisor to the President. By the time Bach finished, I knew about something major happening with NASA, the Air Force, and the Lockhead Martin Skunk Works. Tabby was rubbing my back and Joan Jett was singing about hating herself when something clicked.

"Tabby, I got an idea." I pushed my chair to my work computer and started searching through old files. I heard Tabby put a new batch of CDs in the player before I got lost in the words scrolling down the screen. Then I found it, an article by Dr. Jorge on the dynamics of change in a social system.

Chapter 15
Meeting

"Mr. President. I think it is time for a meeting with Karpinen. He has known about our surveillance for months."

"Okay. Why don't you meet at NASA headquarters? It would be reasonable that he will show up there. We can sneak you past the press easy enough."

"I'm sorry sir but we did a full psychological review of Karpinen. Everyone agrees that it would be best to meet him on his own ground. We need his expertise and he knows it."

"Can you make it out of Washington without being spotted by the press?"

"I have worked out a plan. I will be going to Dulles where two planes will be waiting. One plane will go to Edwards and the other will go to Grand Forks. A car will meet the plane at Edwards taking my double to the Dryden Flight Center. Another car will meet me at Grand Forks and drive me to Karpinen's farm. To throw the press off I will return two days later by way of the Airbase in Duluth. The two planes will meet again at Wright Patterson and I will fly back to Washington."

"Isn't that a little complex?"

"We have more than the press to mislead. The Russians and everyone else in the world are still spying on us."

"Okay but bring a couple of experts with you. I want nothing to go wrong. According to your reports, Dr. Jorge seems to have the best handle on Karpinen and Dr. Schmitt from Argon is the only scientist that I can understand."

"I can make the arrangements."

***

The three crows were back sitting on the power lines. Move-over had found a nice spot on the bookshelf and was watching me from the living room. A car pulled up with four men in it.

"Tabby. They are here. It looks like three will be coming in. Any questions about the plan?"

"Go soak your head. I'm ready. Make sure you are."

I pulled open the door before they could knock. "Come in. Have a seat."

"Thank you Mr. Karpinen. I am..."

"No intros. Now just sit and get comfortable. Anyone want something to drink? It has been a long drive."

"How do you know about the drive?"

"Come on Mr. Riley. The nearest airport that will land a plane large enough to fly you from Washington and is also large enough not to attract undo attention is two hours away. And I bet you landed in either Minneapolis or Grand Forks, both of which are even farther."

Schmitt asked for some coffee. I could tell Riley was not happy about it but there was nothing he could do. "Tabby, would you keep these gentlemen company while I make some coffee?" Tabby started in with small talk keeping them busy and off balanced. The coffee was soon finished. There wasn't a table near any of the men so they had to balance the cups and saucers on their laps while I passed out sugar and creamers. I felt it was time for my first move when Riley tentatively balanced the cup and saucer on the arm of his chair.

"Mr. Riley. What have you found out about the alien?" Dr. Jorge must not have known about the creature because he spilled some coffee on his lap. The disturbance gave

Riley a few extra minutes to plan an answer.

"What alien?"

"Come on Mr. Riley. How can we even start if you won't answer the simplest questions?"

"I don't know what you are talking about."

I switched to Dr. Jorge. "Doctor, what do you think? Mr. Riley here was caught in a lie and he insists on holding on to it. You see doctor ... A few months ago they found a body of an alien creature just down the road from here. And I am not talking about an alien who crossed the Canadian border. I am talking about a creature with a biological structure that was not formed on this planet.

"Am I right Mr. Riley?"

"Okay. You are right."

"Finally. How do the genetics differ?"

"No chromosomes but the creature did have DNA and RNA. Most of the gross features were surgically constructed. How did you know about it?"

It was time to give them something. "Who do you think killed it? It came here wanting to eliminate me before the big demonstration. I objected to being killed most strenuously."

Riley seemed to go into a state of shock as he tried to coordinate the new information. I let him sit and talked to Jorge about social dynamics. Tabby took on Schmitt with a discussion about our experiments. Riley broke into our talk, "Excuse me."

"Yes."

"Do you know why it tried to kill you?"

"It is pretty obvious. The creature didn't want us to learn about gravity control at this time. Mr. Riley, you are the acting National Security Advisor. You need to do better than that."

"Are they going to try to kill you again?"

"That I don't know. My gut feeling is yes. A more important question for you is, 'Are they going to try do something about the whole planet since the gravity cat is out of the bag, so to speak?'" At that Move-over decided to put in his own comment with a loud meow. Dr. Jorge again spilt his coffee but this time it was cold.

"Why didn't you tell us right away?"

"Would you have believed me? Besides I bet you are already putting up a space defense."

"How do you know?"

"Dr. Jorge should be able to explain. Everything you need to know is out there. The increased work at the Skunk Works, Edwards, Dryden, and so on. All of the changes over the last few months add up." We finally got down to a give and take discussion.

It was a warm late fall day so I went outside to grill some sausages for lunch. The nice thing about living in the country is that you can get the best farm products. These sausages came from a local processor. They were both very tasty and juicy. Hot juices burning the chin and splattering the face will keep the men off balance and telling more than they wanted to. The crows were still there. I fed the driver before bringing the rest of the sausages in.

Tabby had Schmitt in an apron dicing onions and Jorge setting the table. Riley had been standing in a corner until Tabby shoved a pitcher into his hands and told him to pour the iced tea. When we sat down, the suits from Washington didn't look like suits anymore. Schmitt was still tearing from the onions. Jorge had two big coffee stains on his shirt and Riley just looked crumpled. Move-over, sensing an opportunity, jumped on Riley's lap and tried to take a bite out of his sausage.

"Move-over. You know better. Come over here and I will give you a piece." The purring started before he got down from the lap. "Be careful. It's hot."

"Meowwwerow."

After lunch, Tabby had them doing dishes. Riley was wiping.

"Can we put some guards in your home?"

"No. If the aliens do come back, the guards would be

killed. Keep them where they are now. That way they will have a chance to survive."

"But how can you handle it alone?"

"You ever hear the military term, point man?"

"No."

"When a patrol goes out in enemy territory they send out a point man. He is the *eyes* of the patrol. He finds what is out there. A point man can't do his job if he is surrounded by the rest of the patrol. He has to be out in front or else both he and the patrol will not make it. I've been walking point for the last year. I can handle myself if that is all I have to look after."

Riley looked at me, his face wide with shock. Slowly, he nodded and changed the topic.

***

"Mr. President."

"Yes Thomas."

"Daniel Karpinen is smarter than we thought. He has known about what we were doing all along. He has been controlling us."

"Damn. I hate being used. Do we have options?"

"Not really, sir. In fact, he told us that we might just be facing either a raid by aliens trying to kill him or a full-scale attack.

"We need to contact the Russians, Chinese, and our allies because if we are attacked we can't have a local war starting by mistake.

"God. What have we come to, thinking of global conflict as a local war? How much time do we have?"

"I don't know and I don't think Karpinen does. But he did start direct talks with us. I think something has to start soon."

"Call General Holcum and I want a meeting of the joint chiefs as soon as we can quietly arrange it. Oh yes. I want Holcum and Scott to go to the War College and have them start setting up scenarios for war games."

"Yes sir."

"Tom, have you thought about what will happen if this is all a mistake?"

"Yes. But what if it isn't?"

Chapter 16
Preparations

"Captain Ree. When do you think you can place the remotes?"

"Our long range sensors indicate that as long as we don't draw attention to our ships we can make the deliveries unnoticed. Which remotes do you want to send Commander?"

"I would like to start with the 30 millimeter creepers. We can add the larger remotes after we get the first information back from the creepers."

"I will send the high protector and the landing vehicle to near orbit on the planet as soon as the 30 millimeters are loaded. The landing vehicle will make a low pass over the site just before dawn planet time. The satellite that we are on will have set in the night sky by then and the lander should be virtually invisible to the inhabitants."

Science specialist Uubee was able to lock on to thousands of electromagnetic sources. The computers were working on translating the signals into the User dialect but so far only patterns were being cataloged. It would take a section of known translation to find the key. Uubee had again begged Commander Zblot to send a team to obtain one of the remote sensing devices that the recordings talked about. A TV, a radio, even the object called a phone could be enough to provide the key to translating the electromagnetic signals.

The members of the assault team were sitting in front of

viewers linked to cameras on the high protector. Grup kept grunting and pointing to the large vehicles traveling on continent spanning pathways. Trreee's mouth would open and close whenever a new variety of flying object would appear. Ed soon stopped watching and started to worry. Nothing at first on the view screens bothered him. Everything seemed so normal, until ... Ed noticed the chaos. Large sections of the planet had few if any artificial vehicles while others had enormous pathways built just for vehicle use. It would be normal for the empty sections to be filled with the harvesting of food substances. But that did not seem the case on this planet. There were just large sections of the planet that were at a different technological level than the others. The climate was extreme. Temperatures easily varied from 100 degrees above the freezing point of water to 100 degrees below. Large expanses of water were interrupted by an assortment of landmasses. Thousands of kilometers of the landmass seemed to be ringed with volcanoes. Huge storms turned up the oceans. This was a planet of extremes.

Ed said, "Boys. Look carefully at the planet. What does it remind you of?"

After a long pause Grup replied, "By *The Hell of the Lost of Debon!* It looks like a military training planet. This place couldn't have been terra-formed could it?"

"I looked at the original planet surveys. There was no indication of planet manipulation. It never occurred to me until I saw the actual planet that a whole population of intelligent life could evolve on a planet this extreme.

"I need to talk to Commander Zblot at once. This place is going to be dangerous."

It took four time cycles before the commander had time to talk to Ed.

"Team Leader Ed, I understand your worry but don't you think that the Chameleon would have noted the similarity of the planet to a military base."

"Sir. Only military planets have all of these extremes in

one location. Infiltrators such as the Chameleon train on a planet, go to a command ship, and are debriefed while traveling to another planet. Military training planets are of two types. The first are basic training camps and the second are specialized training facilities. This is a basic training type planet. An example of most usable planet types can be found on one planet. Only those infiltrators that are assigned to military commands set foot on training planets. I checked the Chameleon's records. The Chameleon went straight from initial training into second and first contact infiltration."

A large dark object sped through the night sky. The only noise was the rushing of the wind as the object cut through it. Over a lonely section of woods, doors on the object opened and thousands of 30-millimeter pellets fell free. A total of 5,832 pellets fell from the sky over 10 square kilometers of woods. 1,234 of the objects hit the earth and remained still. The 4,598 remaining objects unfolded tiny legs. 357 were unable to unfold all six of their legs. 238 of the objects crept away from the landing site in random directions. But 4,003 turned southeast for the 10 kilometer walk to the isolated farmhouse. The six tiny legs moved the 30-millimeter objects southeast using 1-millimeter steps.

Things started to go wrong immediately for the 4,003 tiny remotes. 987 were washed away two hours into the trek when a spillway at a local beaver dam flooded an empty streambed. A small herd of frolicking deer tore though the marching machines leaving 456 crushed little bodies. When the full morning sun lighted the forest floor, the smaller creatures attacked the marching throng. A swallow would swoop down snatching a remote climbing a fallen tree. A raccoon sat for hours grabbing a creeping remote, pulling its legs off, washing it and trying to eat the metal tidbit. Squirrels would grab a remote and stack it in a hollow with the rest of their nuts.

228 of the original 4,003 made it to the edge of the field next to the farmhouse after a full day of walking. 97 made it

across the field. A car pulled in front of the farm crushing 20 creepers. Hurried steps accounted for 5 more. And then came the crows. The last small creeper climbed a tree next to the farmhouse. It anchored itself to the tree and raised the back of its shell making a perfect parabolic transmitting dish. The first image of the farmhouse made it to the Users ship before it was replaced by a large yellow slitted eye followed by a meow and a crunching of metal.

Captain Ree said, "I think we will have to try tomorrow night with the 25-centimeter drones."

***

Captain Sam McHenry loved the Air Guard. The Air Force was okay but with the Guard he flew civilian planes every day and was still able to take an F-16 for a joy ride at least once a week. The guard unit he was in, the 148th in Duluth, was one of the best. The 148th had a history of beating regular Air Force units in war games. To top it off since the 148th was part of the Air Force rapid deployment group to Europe; he had a chance for an all expense paid three-week vacation in Germany and England next year. McHenry just hoped he wouldn't be in a deployment to the Middle East. He had been in the Gulf before and didn't have any fond memories of the place.

McHenry knew something big was up. The 148th was ordered to have two ready planes fueled, weapons loaded and pilots suited prepared for immediate take-off, twenty-four seven. The briefing that just finished had a story about Colombian drug dealers using stealth aircraft purchased from the Chinese based on an original Russian design being used for deliveries in Minnesota. But why was a squadron of F-22 Raptors just moved to Grand Forks? And why were they installing those super secret missiles, AIM-X12Cs, under the wings of his Falcon? The AIM-X12C was an intelligent missile with optical, radar, and heat sensors onboard and guidance feed from the F-16's radar or an AWACs. It was a huge missile that rivaled the AIM-54C Phoenix in size. All that firepower couldn't be for some two-bit Colombians. And why the special heads up for that private experimental aircraft, YS1? Something definitely wasn't kosher.

Well at least he would be able to do some flying against the F-22s. The squadron was scheduled to start a training rotation with the F-22 squadron this week. Most of the dogfights were to take place over Lake Superior. The Big Lake was a deceptive hunting ground, which he had used to his advantage in past war games with other fighter groups.

The engineers from Sandia Labs finished the final checklist on the six-meter rail gun they constructed at the White Sands Missile range. The part of the installation that took the longest was getting the huge power supply required for charging the rail's capacitors to work without blowing transformers or relays. The rail gun project had languished since the late 1980s. It had been part of Regan's Star Wars plans until it became obvious to even Congress that no one had the money to construct the system. The orders to finish the gun and install it a White Sands had surprised everyone at Sandia. The project had never completely stopped over the years. NASA had kept a minimum research funding on the project with an eye towards using a rail gun to shoot micro satellites into orbit. The Sandia engineers were surprised that nearly immediately the Air Force personal manning the gun started test firing at a target down range.

Two Boeing 747s started flying between the Dryden Flight Center in California and the Marshall Center in Huntsville. The planes would take lazy circuitous routes across the country. Hidden inside the planes were the most powerful portable lasers ever developed.

All US military units were placed on DEFCON IV. A small select group of Air Force, naval, and army units were placed at DEFCON III. A few reporters caught wind of the increased readiness of the military. But a low level Pentagon briefing told of joint exercises with NATO, Japan, and the Russians. The news services in those countries received similar reports. The small handful of reporters who were still digging into the increased military readiness were brought to the Pentagon. They were told they could view the war games from units inside the exercise but they would have to move in with the units and maintain a complete communications blackout until after the exercises. Only three reporters accepted. One reporter was sent to White Sands, another to Camp Ripley, and the last to Grand Forks. There they sat in isolation through most of June wishing they had never accepted the Pentagon's invitation to the exercises.

***

The 25-centimeter drones faired no better than the 30-millimeter. Commander Zblot complained to Science Specialist Uubee, "What is happening to the drones?"

"We still don't have enough information on the planet or its inhabitants but similar incidents have been reported on other planets. It was discovered, after the fact, that an oil used or a sound made by the mechanicals attracted the local fauna. You could send in the drones large enough to discourage attacks from the local wildlife or send in the assault team. Either choice has risks. Do we even know if the Chameleon's last target is still at the site?"

"No we don't..."

"We will have to send in the assault team. The Chameleon was able to integrate into the local planet so the team's infiltrators should be able to do the same. This will be dangerous so I want you to spend the next few cycles going over every detail of the insertion with the assault team members. Make sure they understand the parameters of the foray. They are to grab all humans at the site for interrogation on board the ship. If that is not possible, they are to kill everyone there and destroy the building. And yes Uubee. If there is time and room, they can bring back your scientific trinkets."

"Thank you Commander. We need those trinkets to finish the translation of the equations."

Chapter 17
Raid

I saw more birds today on the power lines. Since we talked to National Security Advisor Riley, a small flock of birds took up the watching of the house from the power lines that followed the country road. We had finished YS1 tests a few months back. The grad students had left at the end of the spring semester. For the last month I had spent time every day trying to talk Tabby into staying at her home. During the last few days, Move-over and all the other creatures around the farm seemed more on edge. Their unease transferred to me.

Tabby left for home hours ago. I tossed in bed until Move-over climbed on top of me and started kneading. His claws just touched my skin through the blankets. I got dressed and went outside. It was a crisp dark night. The stars seemed bright enough to read by. On the northern horizon a ribbon of pale blue green light danced from east to west and back again. The northern lights were bright and thin tonight. The thickness of the ribbon only reached a third of the way up from the northern horizon. I stood and watched the dancing lights.

I felt Move-over weave between my feet rumbling a tune as he rubbed his shoulders and chin against my ankles. Move-over stopped his weave. A small black dot appeared between the Borealis and me. The dot skittered across the light, dipped down to the dark horizon. A few minutes later the dark dot reappeared in front of the pale blue green light and shot straight up into the night sky. An orange glow started in the eastern sky. The dark night faded in a red glow as the sun slowly rose in the east.

Tabby and I spent the day combing the woods north of the farm. The animals still watched but something was wrong with them. The whole forest seemed on the move. Deer were prancing down their trails. Squirrels were chattering alarm in every quarter of the forest.

During the day, the air became warmer and heavier. The sounds became muffled. A dark stillness settled across the woods. Dusk was starting to fall when we headed back to the house for supper. We hurriedly ate. I couldn't stay put in one place so Tabby and I walked out into the night. Muffled explosions drifted across the open field from the woods. There was a gunfight happening in the dark.

**

Ed went over the plan one last time with Commander Zblot. The landing ship will place the team 17 kilometers away from the farm in the most isolated area within a day's walk from the last site the Chameleon was known to be heading to. The team will spend the day getting acclimated to the new planet and working their way closer to the farm. After dark, the team will capture or kill everyone at the targeted farm. They will then use the dark to make it back to the landing site and removal to the command vessel. Captain Ree and the crews of the landing ship and high protector agreed upon emergency codes and procedures in case things went wrong with the original plan. Ed triple checked everyone's understanding of the codes and procedures. The one thing all of Ed's long years of training had instilled was that nothing worked as planned.

The insertion was flawless. The two scout/infiltrators disappeared into the woods at opposite ends of the drop site. Trreee went up into the highest nearby growth. Grup limbered up the heavy weapons. Ed stepped back into the woods using a long viewer. Grup and Trreee were nearly invisible. The two scouts were invisible. The camouflage suits were correctly adjusted to the planet. The team easily acclimated themselves to the sounds and creatures of this new planet. The experience of dozens of planetary insertions made the acceptance of the shades of colors, smells, textures and tastes of the new planet immediate. Within minutes, the team was able to start isolating the movement and actions of the stray animals that passed by.

By late afternoon, the team moved closer to the farm.

***

All day Felix sensed the change in the woods. He had seen Karpinen and his girlfriend fade into the woods that morning. The caution they used walking into the woods was what first set his nerves on edge. But it was the actions of the small forest animals later in the day that made him check the action on his sniper's rifle. Todd and Sam for the first time noticing the changes in Felix checked their weapons as well.

Felix didn't relax when he saw Karpinen come back from the woods with his girlfriend. Instead of crossing the field from the woods, they walked along a fence line. He did not know how the two did it but they seemed to fade into the few scraggily pieces of brush that marked the property line. Suddenly, the observation post seemed too exposed. Using hand signals, Felix indicated to Todd and Sam to follow as he walked deeper into the cover of the forest.

Felix was following a logging road. In the quiet evening, their footsteps crackling the undergrowth were the only sounds they heard. Felix stepped around a tree and before him stood an old man with a 30-30 rifle. He knew immediately it was Karpinen's Uncle Ben.

"Shhhh. They are coming. Follow me. I will place you."

Felix took ten seconds to think it over. Even if he never saw the old man before, he somehow knew that he had to trust him. He got on his radio.

"Look-out to Base. Look-out to Base."

"Base to Look-out, what do you need Look-out?"

"Base. We have trouble. There are unknowns advancing on target through the woods. We are moving to intercept the unknowns. Suggest full support."

"Look-out. Can you give details?"

"Not now, Base. Intercept imminent."

The old man moved Felix off the trail behind the roots of a fallen tree. The old man then placed Todd and Sam farther up the road. He hurried back.

"You've got a good field of fire here. I told your boys what to do. There will be a point man leading. When he gets across from you, Todd will call for them to halt. If they don't, you will have to take out the point and help Todd and Sam with the middle. I will take out the last man in the column."

Before Felix could offer a comment, the old man was gone. Felix looked over his men and the trail. The old man had made a perfect placement for an ambush. Todd was hidden behind a tangle of trees that had fallen in mass. Although he was close to the logging road, the mass of tree trunks made a frontal move on his position virtually impossible. Sam was farther along the road and only had a large tree in front of his position but he had a small pocket in the ground that was deep enough to protect him. Every one of his men could support the others with open lines of fire. And they had a clear view, even in the dusk, of nearly one hundred yards of road.

The first man Felix saw had some sort of camouflage suit on. It was the best suit Felix had ever seen. The only way he was able to follow the man was when he moved. The man stopped for a brief instant in front of Todd's position and Felix lost him in the background until he moved again. The man came closer and Felix finally heard his soft steps through the undergrowth.

Three more followed but they were not men. All three

had on the same camouflage suits as the point but there the resemblance ended. The lead in the following group was large with six limbs. The second person, thing, or whatever was huge. It was about the size of an upright walking six-legged Kodiak bear. The final creature in the group also had six limbs but in addition it had wings. Although the last creature seemed too large to fly with its wings, it did glide from tree to tree. Two sets of legs would grasp the trunk of the tree while the creature surveyed the surrounding woods holding a lethal looking device in its last set of limbs. All the creatures were clutching devices that were obviously weapons.

Todd yelled, "Stop. Police. Put down your weapons." And all hell broke loose.

Felix was so astounded by what he had seen he had lost track of the point. He tried to find the creature amid the sounds of gunfire, small explosions, and some wild ripping sounds. Finally, Felix heard a rustle of leaves and found the point creature. It was trying to circle behind Todd's position. Felix pressed the trigger on his rifle and emptied the clip into it.

He looked back down the trail and at first saw nothing. The ripping sound came again and a trail of torn vegetation traveled from a point near where he last saw the creatures to where Todd was hidden. Felix loaded a new clip into his rifle and placed scattered shots around the origin of the ripping sound. A staccato blast of sound came from somewhere overhead followed by a scream of pain from Sam. Felix lost in the horror emptied his clip into the trees. A scream that could never have been made by a creature living on earth today echoed through the woods from the trees beyond. Felix knew that the old man had struck. Something hit him hard in the side. Felix put another clip in his rifle. There was nothing. Nothing moved. No sound drifted through the woods. Just the smell of smoke, ozone, and blood.

The radio message from Felix caused an organized

chaos to occur. Harry Zimmerman and Major Stanley Burrows got on secure phones and started calling for help. John Smith, the CIA man, got the remaining personnel together. They suited up with flak jackets and weapons, piled into two cars, and headed towards the farm.

Major Burrows' calls were to a Delta team waiting at a hotel in a town 15 miles away. Both the Grand Forks and Duluth Airbases had ready planes waiting for a possible call from the Major. The two F-16s got airborne first with the F-22s only minutes behind. The first three calls were just alerts to the ready teams but with the Camp Ripley call Burrows insisted on telling the captain in command of the Marines, good luck.

Zimmerman's calls activated the national space defense network that Riley and the Joint Chiefs had designed over the last few months. From Ellsworth Air Force Base, Rapid City, South Dakota two B-1 B Lancer bombers and an AWAC plane were launched. The B-1 B's flew to maximum altitude and launched four orbital rockets each. Each rocket housed three satellites. Twelve of the twenty-four satellites were designed to aim lasers sent from the Boeing 747's and a new military satellite launched four weeks earlier. The remaining twelve satellites were kinetic kill weapons powered by gravity spheres. They rested in orbit waiting for NASA space control in Houston to give them a target.

The most unusual occurrences from Zimmerman's call weren't the military activations but a secret program that Riley and the NSA had pushed past the Joint Chiefs of Staff. Riley knew that the military was great finding known enemies and destroying them. But in this case they were looking for the unknown. With his time in the NSA, Riley noticed that everyone always had problems with the SETI, Search for Extra Terrestrial Intelligence, programs and the big radio telescopes. Those radio telescopes seemed to find every secure signal the NSA used. Riley decided that they needed the brainpower and the technical ability of the nation's radio telescopes behind them in a crisis situation.

He recruited personnel at Ohio State University's Big Ear Project, Cornell's Arecibo, MIT's Haystack near Westford, Massachusetts, the NRAO at Green Bank, West Virginia and Tucson, Arizona, Caltech's projects in Mauna Kea, and the AST/RO at the Amundsen-Scott South Pole Station. Funding for new communication links to NASA and, in turn, to the US military was given in the disguise of modernization grants. And funding was found to bring all the radio telescopes back into service with the addition of a few new Argus Arrays.

With the knowledge that a raid in Northern Minnesota had to be supported by craft in near earth orbit overhead, the telescopes got into action. MIT's Haystack Observatory got the first indications. The aliens were using focused radio transmissions to minimize the ability for being found but even focused signals will scatter when hitting atmospheric and other free floating molecules in space. Haystack caught lines of scattered radio signals going from a point in space to a site closer to the earth surface and another fainter line of signals going into space. The Green Bank and Tucson telescopes zeroed in on the radio source giving a triangulation for a precise location of the near earth signals and the deeper space signal source. Using the location, the AWAC, now flying over North Dakota, was able to plot were the low flying stealth craft was and guide the four interceptors to it. The AWAC was also able to bring the White Sands rail gun into action to handle the near earth orbiting craft.

The other end of the radio signal was plotted to a crater shadow on the surface of the moon. The dry air of the South Pole permitted AST/RO at Amundsen-Scott to get the first locational fix. Mauna Kea and Arecibo soon followed. The next step waited till the laser aiming and kinetic satellites from the B-1 B's received coordinates from Houston.

Captain Sam McHenry flew his F-16 as close to the ground as possible. His wingman Lieutenant Jamison was a little slow following his lead. McHenry had started flying with A-10 Warthogs. Warthogs survived modern electronic warfare's faster more maneuverable foes by getting lost in the ground clutter. McHenry instinctively sought the safety of the ground. It saved his life today. A flash of light and Jamison was gone. The IFF signals -- Identification Friend or Foe -- in his HUD display told him that two F-22s were coming in from Grand Forks but he had nothing showing on the plane that took out Jamison.

Suddenly, there was an infrared source followed by a series of explosions on the ground. McHenry launched the AIM-X12C and jinked to the right. Three explosions happened in the air near where the infrared source had been. McHenry's radar suddenly showed a large object falling from the sky. Another series of explosions. The IFF signals showed that both of the F-22's were gone. McHenry dropped lower to the ground clipping the top of a large white pine. What the hell was happening?

A five man Delta team driving from a nearby town to the farm saw the explosions in the sky and thought the same thing. A company of Marines and one scared reporter took off from Camp Ripley in a string of helicopters. The lead chopper saw the explosions. The pilot swallowed hard and picked up speed.

In White Sands the rail gun was loaded and ready. The AWAC, now between Bismarck and Grand Forks, was feeding in target information to the rail gun. The high orbit ship that took out the F-22's with what looked like a laser was 235 kilometers above the earth. The craft was holding stationary above where the first craft had been destroyed by missiles. When the orbiting enemy craft firing started, it became visible to the heat and energy sensors on the AWAC, which was able to make fine course corrections for the rail gun.

The rail gun fired a 2.75-kilogram block of metal with a muzzle velocity of nearly 10 kilometers per second. The outer shell of the metal projectile was aluminum composite.

Lines were etched in the outer shell letting the aluminum fall away when the air friction melted the metal. Inside the shell was a 2-kilogram tungsten rocket steerable dart. The first projectile was fired. Forty seconds later the projectile was in outer space with a velocity of 6.31 kilometers per second. Three seconds later the projectile reached apogee and started its acceleration to the alien craft. The rail gun had a recharge rate on its capacitors of 30 seconds. In the next five minutes, it fired a volley of ten rounds. The first dart missed the craft but the craft's onboard sensors told the pilot they were being attacked. The pilot jerked his ship up from the planet. The second and third darts missed. But the fourth hit the craft. The trajectories of both the craft and the projectile resulted in a combined release of 75.63 megawatts of energy. The fifth, sixth, and eighth darts passed through the debris field turning up the residue of the already destroyed vessel.

The guidance satellites had finally climbed into position. Both Boeing 747s were now in the air. The two lasers on the 747s and the one laser on the laser platform satellite fired. The three beams bounced off three satellites and hit the crater shadow on the moon. Before the next laser beams were fired a responding energy beam leapt into space destroying the first three satellites. The lasers now fully recharged bounced off three other satellites. This time there was no response. A third volley into the crater's shadow and no following response. The lasers held fire waiting to see if the target moved before the kinetic satellites could arrive.

The kinetic satellites had the strongest spheres made by man but the limiting factor was the battery life on the spheres and not the force. NASA's computers started their calculations. The computers said an acceleration of 9.873 gravities was needed to start the trajectory to the moon. The twelve kinetic satellites hit the edge of the crater 53.754 minutes after the last laser volley. They all missed the spacecraft. The twelve penetrated into the moon's crust to its core vaporizing and melting kilometers of rock. Twelve lava plumes erupted from the impact sites. The plumes lasted for 29 seconds before a huge volcanic explosion blew out the side of the crater. Millions of metric tons of molten rock filled the edge of the crater.

***

Ed was caught by surprise by the ambush. He had expected trouble by the tree line and not inside the woods. Grup got the first shot off. There had been many attempts to create energy weapons for troops in the field but nothing was ever found to replace the killing power of the simple projectile weapon. Grup's heavy weapon fired hundreds of explosive darts in short bursts with a ripsaw sound. Grup's bust tore a hole in the bulwark in front of the voice that told them to stop. There was a blast from behind and Grup went down. The tattletale monitor that hung next to Ed's eyes showed that Grup was seriously wounded and that the lead scout was dead. Ed heard Trreee's weapon firing from overhead. He rolled over to the wounded Grup and took his heavy weapon from him and started firing at the bulwark. Projectiles slammed into Grup's body and one hit Ed hard passing through his body between the second and third sets of limbs.

A loud scream echoed through the woods and the tattletale told him that only he and Trreee were left alive. Ed whispered into the communicator for Trreee to back away from the fight and circle around behind the bulwark of trees. Ed kept a slow covering fire over the positions of the attackers trying to give Trreee time to swing behind. He felt lightheaded as the blood loss started to weaken his body. Something about the turned up dirt penetrated the battle haze that ruled his mind. The smell. What about the smell? The dirt smelled like the field that he played disk ball on before he went into military training. Something hit him again.

The landing ship flew in close to the ground when the

telemetry on the assault team showed them taking casualties. It flew over the conflict area but the undergrowth masked the fighting. It became obvious that assault team was lost. The landing ship circled high and armed three chemical bombs. The copilot saw a fast approaching plane. He used a chemical laser to destroy the plane and ran a sensor sweep for any other approaching craft. The copilot had to cut the sweep short as the pilot swooped down to launch the rocket guided bombs on the farm buildings. The pilot saw a vehicle pull up to the buildings just before the house, garage, and shed disappeared in an explosive haze of dust and fire. The copilot started his sensor sweep again. He was just in time to see the three antiaircraft missiles before they impacted the ship.

The high protector observed the destruction of the landing ship. Its sensors pinpointed the position of two of the three attackers, which were destroyed instantly. The other attacker would only appear for second on his screens before being lost in the folds of the planet's surface. The high protector started to lower its orbit trying to lock on to the attacker who got away when the first rail gun projectile passed by. The ground assault was forgotten as the pilot fought for his life.

Commander Zblot and Captain Ree watched the raid dissolve into disaster. Uubee and his assistant watched what was happening from the secondary monitors in the crew quarters. They sat in stunned silence as first the assault team, the landing ship and the high protector all were destroyed in sequence. Their first indication that they were under attack occurred with the lasers smashing into the open viewing and remote sensing ports, burning out all outside communications. The ship's automatics fired a response but the armored doors on three of the eighteen ports refused to close. The second laser volley hit the ship. Then a third.

"Captain Ree. What hit us?"

"According to the readouts it is some sort of phased energy beam. They can't damage the hull of the ship but they wasted the sensing ports."

"Can they be fixed?"

"I am getting damage control reports now ... It will take just a little over three standard time units to finish the repairs. The sensors can be replaced in just under one time unit but the three jammed doors will take the bulk of the work."

"Good. Before light returns to the landing site we can avenge our comrades by blasting the entire region with plasma bombs."

All members of the crew were conscripted to repair the ship or load the bombs in their launch tubes. The last door was being repaired and the last bomb was being loaded when the ship was rocked with an explosion.

"How did they hit us? What did they use? We are days away from their planet with their best technology."

"They must have found out how to use their gravity control."

"What did they use?"

"There is no radiation ... It must be a kinetic weapon. We should be safe. *Debon*! We are being covered in lava!"

"So what. We are exposed to higher temperatures when we go near a star to travel between space."

"We are in flight then. We shed the energy build up through exhaust ports. We can't shed the energy. The ports are filled with lava."

"Can't we..."

***

Tabby and I were about to run into the woods but Move-over yowled and started scratching at the metal shed that had the flying submarine in it. We looked at each other and thought why not. We climbed into the submarine with Move-over right behind us. I had spent the most time during the YS1's trials with the flight controls while Tabby had worked mostly with the engineers. I climbed into the pilot seat. We weren't planning on being in the air for long so I pushed the power controls as high as they would work near the ground. We were airborne within 50 feet of the main doors of the shed. I somehow knew that if I climbed we would die so I steered the craft into the valley in the treetops that marked the logging roads that crisscrossed the countryside. The wings of the YS1 brushed the treetops while the body of the plane road between them.

I was just about to ask Tabby where we should go when an owl flew across the front of the plane following a crossroad that headed towards where the sounds of the firing we had heard earlier.

"Tabby, do you think we should follow?"

I heard a faint "Yes."

The owl suddenly banked away and ahead of us was another flying creature. Streaks of light erupted from the creature. What were they? Muzzle flashes? I suddenly knew it was trying to kill something in the woods. Uncle Ben? I jammed the controls to full power while aiming at the creature. The computer read the control settings and adjusted the power to the gravity spheres at the front of the plane to full power and turned off the secondary systems along the surface of the wings. The night became darker and the gravity spheres started to whistle. The creature turned in midair. I could see it trying to bring up what looked like a gun. Just before impact everything to the side of creature faded into black. There was crashing and tumbling and finally we were on the ground.

I climbed out of the plane first. The night was silent. I heard my Uncle's voice. "Dan. There are no bad guys left in the woods. We have some wounded men. Come out and help." I followed Ben up the logging road. The leader of the FBI surveillance team was sitting up next to a tree trunk, binding a wound on his side and arm. He looked up. "What about Sam and Todd?"

Ben replied, "Sam is gone. I haven't looked for Todd yet."

I said to the man, "Can you walk?"

He shook his head yes. "Up the road a little ways is a yellow submarine. Tabitha is there. We will meet you there with Todd." The man stared with a blank look on his face. I pointed, "Go up the road." I helped him up. When I turned, Ben was already making his way over a mass of broken trees. Ben was bending over something by the time I caught up to him. It was a man. Half of his face was burnt away and his left arm was missing at the shoulder.

Flashes of light and a rumble through the ground followed by a roar in the air. Ben looked up. "The farm is gone."

The man was alive. Something had burned the stub of his arm keeping the bleeding under control. Ben finished checking him over. "We can move him. I will take the shoulders you lift the feet." We picked our way around the dead fall. We had barely started when there were flashes in the sky followed by more explosions.

The FBI man was sitting in the same position but now his back was leaning against the submarine when we arrived with the wounded man. Tabby was looking over what was left of the flying sub. The front sphere looked like it was crushed from the inside and the wings were just broken stubs. "Tabby. We need to get the men out of the woods. Can we use the sub?"

"The back sphere is working and we have two wing spheres left on each side. If we put the wounded on top of the wings and power up the spheres, we should be able to push everything out of the woods backwards."

"Let's get them on."

Tabby was climbing into the submarine to turn the power on to the spheres when we heard the helicopters. Ben listened. "Marines. We should be safe heading back to the house."

I was pushing on the wing next to the man without the arm. Tabby was on the other side while Ben pushed from in back. The yellow submarine moved easily. The vents on the wing spheres started to whistle. Blood from the wounded man dripped down the wing to the vent. Red strings of bloody air vibrated into the night sky. The melancholy sound from the whistling vents brought back a memory from my childhood. My grandmother would visit and tell stories and legends from Finland. One of the stories was about a mythical man who knew everything but was never able to find a wife or have a family. This man, Vainamoinen, would play and sing beautiful sad songs for the gods and all of the creatures of the earth. In my child's mind, I had always thought of the strings on the Vainamoinen's harp being a sad red in color. The harp Vainamoinen used was called a kantele. I knew I would call the gravity spheres kantele from now on.

We were coming close to the edge of the woods. Ben yelled, "Yo. Marines. Coming in with wounded."

"Who are you?"

"The wounded are FBI. The rest of us used to live at the farm."

"Come out into the open and stop."

We stepped out of the woods and into hell. There was an orange glow coming from where the buildings used to be. Red flares were marking the road and a landing site for the helicopters. Flashing lights from police cars and ambulances strobed just past the next dip in the road. Dark silhouettes ran across the orange, red, and flashing lights disappearing into the darkness of the surrounding fields.

Chapter 18
Rebuilding

I don't know what woke me. It could have been the throbbing headache or the hard ground. I woke trying to figure out where I was. Soft puffs of warm moist air touched my neck and I knew the warmth coming from my side was Tabitha. I moved, the throbbing increased, and claws sunk into my chest. Move-over had been lying on top of me. I opened my eyes and Move-over stared back. I remembered. I left the tent with Tabby and Move-over still lying together.

Outside I could smell the wet burn of what was left of my farm buildings. It was midday. I looked across the farm. The missing buildings made everything look larger. The army trucks parked around the field gave the feeling of being on a low budget movie set. A single crow was sitting on a power line watching. There was less noise than I thought there would be. Men were moving around. Some were examining the destruction, others were moving back and forth with a seeming purpose, and a few stood around on obvious guard duty. I got a few steps from the tent and a young man in green stepped in front of me.

"Sorry, sir. You have to stay here."

I smiled at the young man trying to stand straight and look soldierly. "Kid. I am not a sir. Why don't we just find someone that we can talk to?" I looked at the kid. I hurt too much to push around him but I was cranky enough not to give up.

"I'm Major Burrows. Corporal. You can stand guard. I will talk to Mr. Karpinen."

"Yes, sir."

I started to walk past the Major. "I am sorry sir but you will have to stay here till we are sure it is safe."

"Major. We would be dead or fighting for our lives if it wasn't over. Don't you get it? We just won our first interstellar battle. And like I told the kid. Don't call me sir.

"I need a phone. You either find me one or I will walk to my neighbors."

"Mr. Karpinen you just can't..."

"I can't what?" While the poor Major tried to figure out what to say and do, another man walked up.

"Mr. Karpinen. I am Harry Zimmerman, FBI."

"Good for you. Do you have a phone?"

"Yes. But we would like you to be discreet with who you talk to."

I stood with my hand out until Zimmerman gave me his phone. I dialed Tabby's home. While I was waiting for one of her parents to pick up, I asked Zimmerman, "How is Felix and the other man?"

"They are stable..." I raised my hand stopping the conversation.

"Earl. Daniel here. Tabitha is alright. She is sleeping now ... Yes, there was a bit of a problem... Do you know a good contractor for some fill work and a basement and septic? ... Really ... I'll have Tabby call when she wakes up ... Sure ... Bye."

I looked up and saw the Major and Zimmerman watching me. "What's your problem? I got to get things fixed up before winter. Summers are short around here." I saw Tabby climb out of the tent. I smiled. I knew the two men wouldn't have a chance now that she was awake.

A month later I was trying to make a new trailer house livable when Gertrude, a friend of my mother, came to the door with a casserole. By then everybody knew most of what had happened. Gerti said, "Dan you need to patent your work. I know you are busy here but the Coffee Klutch can handle it for you."

"Gerti. What do you know about what I've been doing?"

"Well when you had your demonstration Oggie decided that aerospace would be a place to put some of our investments in. Well we bought into Lockhead Martin and got control of some proxies ... Anyway we know possibly more about what is being done with your discoveries than you do."

"Okay, Gerti. If I have you take care of my patent rights and business, how much is the Coffee Klutch going to ask for?"

"Ten percent."

Gerti convinced me to let the Coffee Klutch handle my business. I was just about broke. It seems that insurance companies don't payout for acts of war. The U of M still wanted me to work on their research project so they did foot the bill for a new metal shed. This one was insulated and fully wired for telecommunications and industrial power requirements. But the rest of the bills left me with just enough for a used trailer house. It was going to be a cold winter except for the warmth of Tabby and Move-over.

***

Spring was my favorite time of year. It was muddy and frequently cold and wet but it was also spring. I just finished blocking into firewood one of the trees downed in the firefight from last year with my new chainsaw. I sat on one of the blocks absorbing the warm spring sunlight and the small noises of the forest creatures. I sat until the sweat evaporating caused a shiver to travel up my arms. I got out the six-pound maul and started splitting the green wood. I sensed Tabitha walking to me.

She smiled as she swayed into my arms. She buried her face into the base of my neck and inhaled deeply. "What are you doing?"

"I am smelling your sweat."

"What for?"

"Don't you like the smell of me when I sweat?"

I had never thought of it that way before. She was right. There is an eroticism with the aroma of fresh sweat dripping off a clean body. Before I had the time to think more, we were rolling around on the only dry spot of ground. Unfortunately for us, it was also the spot where I had finished blocking the tree. It is fun rolling around in fresh sawdust but you will spend the rest of the day fighting the little wood chips in your clothes and clinging to most unusual crevices of the body.

We were walking back to my trailer pulling at the irritations in both our shorts when I asked, "I am going to start the cabin next month. I want you to look over the plans. You need to make sure everything is there that you want."

"Daniel. Are you asking something of me?"

"I sure am. I just asked you to make sure the cabin has everything you want in it."

"Daniel!" She followed that by reaching behind my back and pulling up on the back of my shorts.

"Okay. Okay. No more violence. I want to marry you. And if you don't want to marry me, I want you to live with me. I just want you."

Laughing she replied, "That's better. I will think about it. But I want to see the plans first. Where did you say you were going to put this cabin?"

I told her about putting the cabin deep into the woods on a small rise. The road back to the cabin would travel past the current trailer and lab buildings. The cabin was going to be on the small size with large windows looking in every direction. But underneath the cabin there was going to be a large complex, a full computer lab, a research lab, library, etc.

Tabby wanted to know how I could afford everything.

When I told her that since my patents were granted, I was making over a million dollars a day, her mouth dropped. "Aren't you afraid I might marry you just for your money?"

"So what. I want you any way I can have you."

The rest of the afternoon was spent in the pleasant task of picking little pieces of sawdust off our bodies.

It was much later and we were standing together in the field watching the star filled sky. My hand had wormed its way past Tabby's clothes and was resting on the warm curve of her thigh. Move-over had followed us out to the field and was weaving a pattern between our legs. Small clouds moved in darkening the stars but not blotting them out completely.

"Do you remember how things darkened when I jammed the controls on the sub to ram that flying alien?"

"I wasn't looking out but I remember something happening to the lights. Could it have been the battery drain under full power?"

"Think back. Was there something unusual about the way the darkness happened?"

"I think your right. It seemed darker when we got off the axis of motion."

"Let's go to the lab. I need some serious computer time."

Since my stereo was destroyed with the farmhouse, all I had for music was a boombox and a dozen CDs that I had purchased over the last few months. Tabby kept the music playing while I waded through the information that I had backed up on secure servers before the attack.

I knew back in high school about Einstein's rubber sheet theory of the universe and gravity. He explained that the universe was like a rubber sheet and every object in the universe was like someone underneath the sheet pulling it down. A planet would make a small dimple in the sheet, a star a larger one. A galaxy would make a large section of the sheet lower than the rest. Anything traveling through the universe would act like a marble being rolled on the sheet. If the marble was far enough away from a dimple, it would travel nearly in a straight line. If the marble was closer, the dimple would bend the motion so it would bend off course. If the marble came too close, it would circle the dimple in orbit and eventually fall into the hole caused by the body making the dimple. Einstein also said that the combined forces of all the objects in the universe would bend the whole universe around itself in a massive curve. Making it possible to go in one direction until you came back to where you started.

Why Einstein's rubber sheet theory got to be so interesting to me in high school was Star Trek. As all nerdy kids in school did, we talked about the latest science fiction TV shows and all those things that made interstellar travel possible, things such as wormholes and tears in the universe. Because the rubber sheet that was the universe was pulled so much by the large gravitational bodies such as stars, the theory goes -- if the bent sheet came close to touching another portion of the bent sheet, you could make a wormhole or even a tear in the sheet and go from one point to another in the universe. An obvious choice to find a wormhole or a tear would be to look for them near large gravitational bodies such as stars or black holes. It is known that black holes have enough gravity to pull even light into them. The gravity we were producing in my kantele was not anywhere near the strength of a black hole but the gradient or the shape of the bent rubber sheet might be similar to being near a black hole. If that was true, the darkening of light we saw might have been because we were on the very edge of making a moving wormhole in space.

I started the process by making pictures of the gravitational gradients near the surface of planets and stars. I then compared the gradient caused by the kantele. Although the total force generated by the mass of the planet was a million times greater than the force of the kantele, the gradient for the planet was different. It was just a factor of the planet taking up so much space. The interesting thing I found was that the gradient near a large object like our sun was close to the gradient caused by the power I fed into the kantele. How could I find out if the gradient was enough to make a wormhole possible?

I ran parallel lines of research. One was with string theories and generalized Big Bang expansion theories. The other was with topography. I was looking for when the points of dichotomy in the equations matched with regions where the topography of a multidimensional universe overlapped.

Nothing was happening. Nothing matched.

Every few hours, Tabby would put on the boombox a rock song and pull me away from the computer for food or rest. She would then shove me back online. I vaguely remember that the kids from U of M were back. This registered to my consciousness when some of the labor intensive sorting of information was completed by them between the times Tabby would drag me away and when I can back.

I was about ready to give up until I realized that what I was looking for were chaos dichotomies. I then had the kids map the equations visually on the computer screens. About a week later, I found it. Sitting in the corner of one of the new string theory equations was a Mandelbrot curve. I had found a dichotomy between spatial dimensions. I continued looking and found two more Mandelbrot curves within another possible string theory and two more Julia sets in a Quantum representation of the Big Bang Theory.

I examined the parameters of when the dichotomies would occur. They all appeared within the same part of the gravitational gradient curve. One of the Mandelbrot curves and one of the Julia sets required a high-energy plasma source to produce the dichotomy. The remaining Julia set needed an extreme velocity. But the two remaining Mandelbrot curves occurred when a constant was varied and there was no way to find out if anything other than the gravitational gradient was required to induce the dichotomy.

Tabby must have bought a new CD because I heard the guitars and voice of Jonny Lang coming from the speakers. I suddenly realized how long I had been sitting in front of the computer as my full bladder started to hurt. Not again! I ran to the bathroom.

***

The quadrant meeting of the Users was called to order. The problem with planet H14-D102 was seventh on the list. The death of the infiltrator known as the Chameleon was noted. But the complete disappearance of the clean-up team after the standard notification of arrival on the uninhabited satellite of H14-D102 was very disturbing. The destruction of the mother ship, the two short range space craft, and all life pods had to have happened nearly simultaneously in order to have all contact severed without a report to regional command. Planet H14-D102 was clearly dangerous despite the early reports from the Chameleon. The Users had survived hundreds of thousands of years of space travel by never fighting an opponent they could not guarantee winning against. Some of the other races they had met in space had considered them cowards but the Users still survived while most of the detractors were now gone. In this quadrant, there were eight planets and five space traveling cultures under quarantine. No travel to those eight planets and contact limited to authorized personal with any of the five space cultures. H14-D102 became the ninth planet and an advisory concerning contact with the natives of H14-D102 was broadcast to all User colonies and spacecraft.

Chapter 19
The Cabin

The cabin was hidden in a grove of pine and fir trees. The road was a narrow track following the old logging trails through the woods in back of the farm. It looked like a small retirement cabin but it cost nearly four million dollars to build. The money had gone into what you couldn't see. The basement of the cabin was four times the size of the cabin itself. The basement was a full research and communications center plus at the insistence of the government a fortified bunker, which the government paid for. The cabin was also where Tabby and I were going to start our honeymoon in three days, six hours, and twenty-three minutes.

I had a load of firewood in the trailer behind my small John Deere tractor. I unloaded the wood in the little shed behind the cabin. I took off my boots and jacket in the mud room across from the woodshed. The cabin smelled new. The kitchen gleamed. The great room tinkled. Winters in northern Minnesota are so cold the air is dryer than the Sahara desert. A few years ago my old publishing company had a big meeting in Portland that I had to attend. Between meetings, I went site-seeing to the formal Chinese garden there. Two things I remembered, the quiet tranquility of the garden and the rich humid air. In the corner of the great room, I took a seven by five-foot spot and had constructed a formal Oriental garden with water trickling off rocks and a small pool surrounded by a handful of small plants. This cabin will never have dry air. Over most of the great room was an open ceiling. The second floor was one large bedroom with a balcony overlooking the great room and pool below.

I sat on the couch listening to the tinkling water. I must have dozed off because it was dark when my eyes opened again. I left the tractor by the cabin and walked back to the trailer I was still living in. The moon was strong but it was still possible to see the stars. An owl flew silently overhead blocking out the stars and moon. I knew something more was out there that I had to find. It was now two days, twenty-two hours, and eleven minutes before the wedding.

***

Thomas Riley didn't like the way the meeting was going. General Holcum, Dr. Schmitt, and Dr. Manning were handling the bulk of the discussion. The two main items of contention were why did Karpinen's space drive keep collapsing and why were the fragments of the alien ship found on the moon made out of a ceramic material stronger than titanium steel and able to withstand the temperatures of a plasma torch. This was the third such meeting that degenerated into an argument.

"Okay, gentlemen. We need to be ready if these aliens come back. What do we need that we haven't tried already?" The silence was a shock after the angry words.

Schmitt finally voiced a reply, "We need Daniel Karpinen here to look over every bit of information we have. And we need him to tell us where to go next."

Holcum, "We can't. We will have no control on him. He has shown us before he just tolerates us."

Major Burrows had been standing at the back of the room. He had been brought in as a liaison between the research work at Karpinen's farm and the current project. "Karpinen might just tolerate us but he has always been willing to help. What would be worse, the aliens coming back before we are ready or Karpinen telling the world about a few of the secrets they don't already know? We all know that the press has printed most of the information we have discussed."

Riley made a decision. "Get me Harry Zimmerman on the line. I want the FBI to bring Karpinen ... Where is the nearest base that we can secure for a meeting of most of the researchers?"

Holcum replied, "Grand Forks is large enough."

"Bring Karpinen to Grand Forks. I also want Ole Swenson there. We need a strong applied engineering presence at the meeting."

***

The small church was packed. My oldest friend from Chicago couldn't make it so Tabitha's brother was my best man. There were a few college friends for Tabitha but the rest of the church was filled with friends of both Tabby's and my parents. Erma and her husband sat up front next to Oggie and her husband Tom. Erma was my mother's best friend and Tom was my father's. Both couples had decided that I needed a parent today so they had kept me busy all morning giving me advice. I am still not sure what they said to me but they did keep me from worrying.

The music started and I saw Tabitha for the first time today. She was beautiful. She gave me the sauciest smile coming down the isle. Her dress was hot. Most brides dress for themselves or their mothers in white lace and frills. Tabby had on a simple white satin full-length dress that clung to her figure. She was fully covered but she would have had only slightly less of her figure revealed if she had worn a bathing suit.

I don't remember much about the ceremony. I do remember that my voice cracked every time I tried to answer the minister. And Tabby was laughing at me every time I stumbled.

The reception was also a blur except for our first dance together. I felt every move Tabitha made through the thin material of her dress. She leaned in close to me and I discover for sure what I had suspected earlier. She had on nothing underneath her dress.

Finally, we were able to leave. We had come in separate vehicles. I parked my pickup away from the church and Tabby parked her car next to the church. Her car was covered in shaving cream and streamers but my truck had been left alone. We took my pickup. We had an escort of one FBI car. The car stopped at the entrance to the farm. Just as soon as we got into the woods, Tabby slid across the seat next to me. When I stopped by the cabin, I pulled her close and ran my hands over her body. She leaned into me and I felt something hard between her legs. Curious, I bunched her dress and slid my hands between her legs. Attached, to the inside of her leg with a garter belt, was a throwing knife. Her hands had found my puukko hanging underneath my arm. We laughed and ran to the bedroom. We made love. Sated for a time, I traced her curves using the cold steel of the knife. After leaving a trail of goose bumps down her back with the hard blade, she pushed me away and we had sex. There is a difference between making love and sex. I am usually exhausted after sex so I fell asleep.

I woke later to the smell of food cooking. I found Tabby in the kitchen. She was wearing my wedding present to her. It was a large dark red silk robe. When she moved, a white limb would flash out from under the darkness. We burnt the food while we had sex on the kitchen counter. Much later, we watched the sky grow light listening to the water tinkling in the great room of the cabin.

Knock, knock, knock.

Tabby had her throwing knife in her hand. She stood to the side of the front door while I opened it. "Felix. Nice to see you've recovered. But what are you doing here?"

"Sorry Mr. Karpinen."

"Daniel."

"Sorry Mr. Daniel ... Dan. But I have been ordered to bring you to a meeting."

"I see the hand of Zimmerman here. Well, was he the one?"

"Mr. Zimmerman was the one who ordered me to come here but he just passed along the orders that came from the NSA."

"This is my honeymoon. You go back and have Harry tell Riley to call me in an hour and to ask me politely to come to the meeting." Felix nodded and closed the door.

"What do you think?"

"You will have to go. They will not let us be until they get what they want."

"It is not just me going. You are going with me."

"I am? Well just how are you going to convince me that I should come?" I had just slipped my hand between the folds on her robe when Move-over announced that he was hungry. He had to wait twenty minutes for his food.

There were three large dark SUVs in the convoy that drove us to Grand Forks. Felix was in the middle SUV with us.

"How are you feeling?"

"I am fine."

"Talkative aren't you."

"Dan, stop teasing the poor man. He is just a peon. He doesn't know anything about what is going on."

"Thank you ma'am."

"Now don't you call me ma'am. My name is Tabby."

"Yes maa... Tabby."

"Now I packed just one dress. Do you know if I need to buy another for this thing we are going to?"

I let Felix suffer as Tabby pumped all the information she could out of him. I had seen her do it before. The lisp in her voice and her hearing aids made the person talk more the he should. This was followed by her sex appeal if she was talking to a man. Before we were an hour into the drive, we knew that the meeting would be with scientists, engineers, and the military. The press would be kept out as well as most of the politicians.

A hanger had been cleared out at the airbase. Riley greeted us at the door and introduced us to the 50 or so men in the conference and explained about the support personal and computer connections. Riley had just started explaining the basic problems when I interrupted.

"We haven't discussed my salary yet."

"What?"

"I am not going to do this for free. And you will need to pay my wife as well."

"Your wife?"

"My wife. She has helped me with most of the work I have done."

I could see Riley hadn't stopped to think what my price would be to help. "How much do you want?"

"I want a spaceship."

"What?"

"I want -- a -- space -- ship. After I fix things up here, I want you to build a spaceship to my specifications. Before you go crazy, think about it. You are going to need to build a completely new line of spacecraft. My ship will be a perfect way to test new designs. It is a no lose situation for the government. My ship will be a perfect foil to hide your own spacecraft development." I could see he was thinking.

"And you Mrs. Karpinen. What is it you want?"

"Call me Tabby. I want the ground and personal support required to take the spacecraft for a spin or two across the solar system and beyond."

"Good going dear. I didn't think about the support."

"I know. Should we set up while they are talking?" Riley had walked to the corner of the hanger with General Holcum and a few other men.

"Sure. Let's get our laptops on line. I'll have Felix bring in the boombox and our luggage."

I was humming along with Fleetwood Mac when Riley

came back with an agreement. A John Williams sound track was playing when I dived into the analysis of the remains of the alien spacecraft. Later, Johnny Horton was put on the box so I knew it was time for lunch. I saw Tabby in an animated discussion with an older fellow.

"Who is your friend?"

"Dear, this is Ole Swenson."

"Of the Skunk Works."

"How did you know?"

"Didn't you know dear? We own a good size chunk of Lockhead Martin."

Ole seemed a little dazed. "How are you doing Ole?" I reached out my hand. We shook and I continued, "Let's eat."

"Oh Felix..." I waited till he looked at me, "Would you tell Riley or whoever is in charge now that there will be a meeting of everyone after lunch."

About twenty were at the meeting. I recognized Schmitt, Manning, Holcum, Scott, and a few others whose names I never learned. I got up while Tabby, using a workstation, put up on four large screens the computerized information I was working from.

"I looked over the forensic data from the alien ship. Now I can't tell you for sure what everything means but I do have a few guesses. First off, I think I know why they attacked."

I waited until the mumbling stopped.

"Most of you have not been working with all of the data that I collected on possible interstellar travel. What seems to have been disseminated is the set of equations that I thought had the best chance of working. There are a number of other possible ways of constructing a wormhole or tear in the structure of the universe. One of them would include using the gravity and energy of a star to construct wormholes between stars. For this to work the spacecraft would need to get very close to the sun. I haven't worked out the possible numbers but my best guess would be less than 25 million kilometers from the sun. For carbon based creatures to live during the transfer between stars you would have to have a heavily armored and heat resistant spacecraft. I believe that these aliens use star hopping for travel between stars. And from the ion residue found by the analysis of the radio telescope data after the attack, an ion drive within a solar system.

"What I think the aliens wanted to do was control the artificial gravity theory that I developed. With the theory they would be able to travel without using ion drives or star hopping. For a time, I think, we can monitor space travel to our solar system by placing monitors in orbit around our sun."

Dr. Manning interrupted. "But that can't be right. We know that we disabled the craft with our laser fire. With travel that close to the sun their ship should not have been affected by our lasers at that distance."

"Do we know if we disabled the ship or just the observation and communication sensors? Both the observation and communication arrays would have to be sensitive to the electromagnetic spectrum. After all, we know they were using the spectrum because the radio telescopes spotted the craft. You would not want to fly a craft for any distance without sensors. If they were destroyed by the lasers, the ship would be crippled until they were replaced. As for the star hopping, sensors could be stored behind armored doors during the phase of the hop where the ship was too close to the sun.

Holcum said, "Okay we think we know how they traveled here. But how would we stop a ship that heavily armored if we needed to?"

"The same way we did this time, kinetic weapons. We could even easily use nuclear weapons near the sun. The radiation would have a negligible affect on the rest of the solar system and the kinetic energy of the explosion should either destroy the ship or throw it into the sun."

Holcum replied, "Good. Now we have a defense."

"Hold it. This is a theory. What we need to do is to try to tear it apart. We need to find out if there are any other explanations of the facts."

Schmitt took over the meeting. "Thank you Mr. Karpinen. We now have a new set of theories to work with. Manning, I want you to try to punch holes in Karpinen's theories. Scott, why don't you try to put preliminary plans for a detection sphere around the sun..."

I nodded to Tabby and we walked away. "Why don't we go for a walk before we start working on why the kantele space drive isn't working?" We hooked our arms together. "Felix?"

"Yes, Daniel."

"We are going for a walk."

I saw Felix talk to the military policeman at the door. Outside, I saw a spot of brown green grass in the distance. We walked to it. When we got there, a big four-engine plane was revving on the runway. We sat on the brown grass.

"Tabby, why did you help me with getting the spaceship?"

"I've noticed the same thing you have. Something doesn't feel complete yet. I have seen you watching the stars at night..."

"You know Ben talks about the responsibility of being at point. I somehow feel responsible. If I hadn't discovered that gravity could be made, I could let it go. But I somehow think it is my task to see this through. I've got to walk point again."

The airplane took off drowning out all talk. During the quiet after the takeoff, we sat next to each other, enjoying the feel of just being together, until the next plane started warming up its engines. Back at the hanger we got to work on what was happening with the kantele when they tried to form a wormhole. The remote test ships had torn themselves apart. Most of the pieces of one of the ships were in the hanger with a duplicate of the original construction. The ship was about two and a half meters long with a large spherical kantele in front. The cylindrical body of the craft housed a large computer and sensor package and in the tail was a small maneuvering rocket. The largest piece of the destroyed test ship was about 50 centimeters long and about 15 centimeters wide. Tabby looked over the pieces while I reviewed the data tapes from the test runs. After two Mozart CDs and one Bach, she came over to my workstation.

"I want to show you something."

"Good. I am getting nowhere with the data."

She brought me to the pieces of the kantele sphere first. She handed me a magnifying glass. "Look carefully at the edges. Now look at the edges of the pieces from the body cylinder." I knew she had found something but I couldn't see it at first. I went back and forth between the two groups of pieces. Finally, I saw it. Most of the pieces on the broken sphere were bent inward while the metal from the cylinder was bent in every direction.

"Let's check the data record again." I smiled at Tabby and pinched her bottom. From the corner of my eye I saw Felix smiling at us.

Back at the workstation we carefully followed the pressure and gravity readings off the kantele sphere. On paper they were all within the tolerances of the construction. But I noticed that there was a flutter in the numbers way down in the fifth decimal place. I highlighted the block of numbers with the cursor.

"Do you see what I see?"

"I sure do."

"Why don't we sleep on it?"

"Sounds good to me."

"Felix. We are ready to go to our hotel room."

"I'm sorry sir ... sorry Daniel. But I was told you would be staying on the base."

"I am not spending a night on an Air Force base, especially not on my honeymoon. We called and made reservations at the Best Western before we left home. All we need is a ride to the motel. And before you ask, I reserved a room across the hall for your men."

It was two days later when we had a solution to the star travel problem. This time the meeting had thirty people in it.

"Okay, I assume everyone has gone over the basic data." I waited until most of the heads nodded. "The kantele sphere is not strong enough for the forces generated with using it as a star drive. The original specifications overlooked a problem with the production of the space drive. The gravity field that is generated has a slight vibration to it. Under most conditions it will not cause a problem until thousand hours or more of run time but under the extreme conditions the vibrations will weaken the sphere enough to permit the gravitational force to crush the sphere.

"The solution is to go back to the original design. Remember the sphere was used to eliminate the contamination of the gravitational field with molecules found in the air and on the nearby surfaces. In space we will not have those problems. We have the added benefit of being able to adjust the parabolic reflector to project the field farther away from the dish so the structural strain will be less.

"As for injecting the field generation with air or some other gas, that might not be necessary with the open design. Once the gravity field is started with an initial push of gas the increased strength of the field generation will pull the scattered molecules in space into the field. If it is not enough we can work on some type of gas injection in a following test.

'The next problem will be the actual generation of the wormhole or tear. There is a chance that at a sufficient velocity the tear will be generated spontaneously. I am hoping that this will work. But we do have the backup with the suspected way the aliens traveled. We can try to inject a plasma flow into the gravitational field.

"Tabby and I have made copies of our notes and

working theories. We will be heading home now. I request that data from the next tests be sent to our lab at the farm and that we start working in adjunct with the rest of the groups on the project."

Tabby and I cuddled for the whole trip home much to the discomfort of Felix and the other man in the SUV with us. I was surprised when we got to the cabin. It felt like home.

I woke to the sun peeking through the windows. Tabby was curled up against my side. From the great room, the sound of trickling water drifted over the balcony. I was warm. I traced the curve on Tabby's back and counted her vertebrae.

"What are you doing? I am still tired. If you want sex, you need to do more than tickle my back."

"I'm thinking. And I just wanted to touch you."

"Wacha thinking about?"

"A few years ago I worked in an office and avoided my boss. I didn't stand up to anyone. I even would run away before confronting someone. How the hell was I able to talk back to those people? How in the world do I have the guts to tell all those PhDs they were wrong? Why did I drive the sub into the flying alien? How was I able to help those wounded FBI men? A few years ago I would have driven past an accident and called an ambulance. How could I have changed so much?"

"I remember reading a story. I can't remember the exact words but it said, 'The difference between a man down the street and a hero is what has happened to him?' You never know what you will do until you face it. But after facing it, you change.

"Do you remember those old re-run western movies and the bit about seeing the elephant?"

"Yup. You never could tell what a man would do until he saw the elephant."

"You now know what happens after seeing that elephant."

I stroked her back softly until she went back to sleep. I watched the sun finish rising through half closed eyes listening to the tinkling water and the soft breaths coming from Tabby.

Chapter 20
Construction Begins

There were a million and one things to do. We never had the chance to finish the two weeks we had scheduled for our honeymoon. The day after we got back Ole called with a problem with the new design. We were forced to open up the U of M lab by the county road and start working on the space drive problems. Tabby was best with the engineering questions while I worked on the theory and ideas.

Four months later the first new kantele star drive was tested. They moved in a new satellite optical telescope just to watch the test. The government had started work on the telescope last year with the idea of using it as a guidance system for their new space weapons. The test cylinder moved like the proverbial bat-out-of-hell. The tracking system on the new telescope nearly didn't follow the probe. As the speed of the cylinder approached 200,000,000 meters per second, the optical telescope lost the image of the cylinder and just tracked a distortion line. The internal clock on the cylinder was timed for one second of travel after the onboard computer sensors decided that the probe had entered a wormhole. After the test, they found the cylinder out past the orbit of Jupiter. The onboard computer had already started the probe's deceleration and its return to earth using its standard gravity drive.

It took another six months before all the details about the test were fully analyzed. Manning, at JPL, proved that the kantele drive was not producing a wormhole but a tear in the fabric of the universe. The distortion line left by the test was because the tear was incomplete leaving the test probe partially in our four-dimensional universe as well as out of it. This was an enormous help with the guidance and measurements of the test probes' flights. Plus there was a good chance that enough of the 4-D universe would get through to the probe that it could be used for inboard guidance of a craft while in the tear.

Tabby took the time after the successful test flight to go over the data that had been compiled by NASA over the years on designing long distance spacecraft. The habitat problem was her greatest concern. Even with a useable star drive, we are still talking of possibly years in space. Food, air, water, and most of all a livable environment had to be constructed. There had to be room for exercise and methods to relax between tasks. Early on, Tabby decided that there would have to be animals on board for both company and a distraction. This added a whole second line of problems with the feeding and maintenance of the animals. She cornered me with questions after a three-hour conference call between Manning, Schmitt, and me on guidance problems. I was happy for the break.

"I need to talk to you about the spaceship."

"Okay, let's get out of here and go for a walk." The trailer that I had lived in now housed a small security team for the lab and the farm. I saw a couple of men leave the trailer and sit in lawn chairs watching us head into the woods.

I waited until I got into the movement of the forest. A deep breath and I was calm. "What did you want to talk about?" My hand crept around her back and found a resting-place riding on her swaying hips.

"On the spaceship we need to recycle air, water, food which means green plants, dirt, insects, bacteria -- a small ecosystem. Plus I felt we needed some animals for companionship if for nothing else.

"Am I right and do we have the room?"

"You are right. We will need at least one cat. In the past, sailing ships had some of the same problems. A cat or even a dog was common on those ships. They even had goats and other farm animals for milk and fresh meat. We will just have to make the room.

"You know we are going to have more room than you might think."

"Why?"

"We can use all of the walls as ground. If we had a ten-meter diameter cylinder that is twenty meters long, we would have over 1,500 square meters of ground. Or ... about a third of an acre."

"I want it large enough to take a walk through the trees."

"Let's plant some apple, plum, and cherry trees."

"Nice. Food plus visual enjoyment."

We walked to the cabin and decided to call it a day. After making love next to the trickling pool, we decided to add that to the plans.

Three weeks later while walking from the cabin to the lab, I notice the animals looking both at me and a specific spot ahead. I felt Tabitha tense. She slipped behind and to the side while I stopped to move some fallen branches off the access road. My puukko was in my hand. Tabby was easing around a tree with her throwing knife out and ready. Two men came out from behind some trees. One had a microphone and the other had a video camera.

"Mr. Karpinen. I am Tony James from News First. We have been trying for weeks to get a comment from you about all the deaths that have occurred worldwide using your artificial gravity machine."

"Camera and sound off."

"Don't you want your response known to the public?"

"Camera and sound off." The TV face on the man changed and he nodded to the cameraman to stop taping. Before either knew what was happening, Tabby came up behind them and double-checked that the equipment was turned off.

"Two questions before you get to ask anything. What deaths are you talking about? And what is this bull about trying to contact me?"

"Ever since you released the information on your artificial gravity devices people have been making them. Over the last two years there have been 35,000 deaths and 80,000 injuries world wide from people using your devices. They range from the spectacular crash of a homebuilt gravity plane into the Chrysler building in New York to the decapitation of an experimenter in New Deli when he turned the power up too high on the gravity device he had built in his garage and a sickle was pulled off the wall. Do you think the courts should hold you libel for these events?"

"Answer my other question. What is this bull about trying to contact me?"

"We called your corporate lawyer about the possible filing of a suit by the builder of the plane that ran into the Chrysler building."

"Really, what is this possible suit all about?"

"The pilot of the plane is claiming that there should have been a disclaimer that you had to be a trained pilot before using your gravity device to power a plane."

"So you are here asking for comments on a suit that hasn't been filed. I bet you were contacted by the lawyer of this pilot. Weren't you?"

"What are your comments about all the deaths and injuries caused by your device?"

"Come with me."

I walked them out of the woods. Felix and his men pulled the reporter and his cameraman aside. While they kept the reporter busy, I called the sheriff's office and asked for Tom. I explained how I had found a reporter and cameraman trespassing on the farm. Tom showed up in twenty minutes.

The FBI men had the two men surrounded. Tom

nodded to them and said, "Are these the ones caught trespassing?"

"Yes."

Tom gave me a wink. "I'll take care of it." He got out cuffs and put the men in the back of the car and their equipment in the trunk. "What do you want me to do with them?"

"Just make sure if they want a comment they come to the lab and ask. I don't want them hanging around inside the property line. It might pay to remind them that people died here less than two years ago.

"How's Oggie? It has just been so crazy out here I haven't had much of a chance to keep up with local events."

"Oggie's fine. She and the other gals are making money. I hear them talking on the phone between the soaps about it. They are talking about throwing a big picnic at the State Park. How about coming?"

"Give me a call with a time and date. Tabby and I will show up."

"What was that? Did you just volunteer me for something?" asked Tabby.

"Just a picnic meal with the Coffee Klutch gals."

"Mom was telling me about that."

"Well bye Tom. I appreciate it."

"No trouble."

***

No one knew how old the Cell was. Records were never kept. But Mikhail Bakunin's *'the passion for destruction is also a creative urge'* and Enrico Malatesta's *'propaganda of the deed'* were both quoted during the indoctrination of a new member using both the original Russian and Italian languages. The rumor was that at least one of those men was personally involved with the forming of the Cell.

The current leader of the Cell used the name Santa. He looked like Saint Nick but he was a true terrorist. That jolly bearded face had watched the pieces of a hundred bodies picked up after the bombs that he had made exploded. All members of the Cell used noms de plume during all meetings and communications. The history of the Cell was peppered with incongruous statements such as Olive Oil drowned the ambassador or Peter Piper blew up the building.

"We need to find a new target. Our actions have been marginalized by the news media over the last few months. The bombing at the economic summit only made the national news for two days. And we were unable to stop the ecumenical peace conference after Juliet was caught poisoning the food."

Hamlet said, "I still think that we should supply equipment and intelligence to eco-groups. With the building evidence of manmade global disaster, everything they do will be reported."

Santa replied, "The Cell has survived because we have chosen to do only one act of terrorism every six months and have done everything ourselves. If we do more, we will become a target of the establishment and every person who knows about us outside the group adds for the chance of betrayal."

Snow White said, "Why don't we do an assassination? We have been concentrating on the big conferences and meetings because of all the media news organizations covering the events. But a well chosen murder will bring the media to us."

Romeo said, "Why not? We have stuck too long with the same events. We need some variety to bring back our *creative urge.*"

Santa cleared his throat. "Okay. Does anyone have an idea for next *passion?*" And looked to Snow White.

"I think the best way is to strike at the current darling of industry, government, and science. We need to kill Daniel

Karpinen. And we need to do it in a spectacular way. The *'propaganda of the deed'* has to be worthy of the target."

With the formal language from the past, the group agreed to the new target.

Chapter 21
Building the Ship

The picnic was just what we needed. Felix and his men looked out of place with their attempt to blend in with civilian clothes. They just couldn't hide the guns and radios. They all insisted on wearing dark glasses so they could observe people without them seeing were they were being looked at.

I didn't feel that old but lately everyone I seemed to be talking to was over fifty. Manning, Schmitt, Ole ... the ladies from the Coffee Klutch were my daily business contacts. The U of M college students never wanted to socialize... For the first time in months there were kids and young adults. Tabby was gone just as soon as we got out of the cars talking to her high school friends. I remembered a few from my high school days but I had left school too many years ago to need to talk to them.

There was one thing about the state park that made it the place to be in the summer. It had a great swimming beach. I had my swimsuit under my clothes. The water was cold enough to send chills through your body but warm enough that you could stay in for an hour at a time.

Kids were splashing. From a dock next to the swimming beach, a group of adults were pulling skiers amid yells and splashes. I got sand in my hair and water up my nose. I felt young again. Tabby came out to join me. We splashed and groped each other under the water. Chilled, we climbed out and laid on our towels absorbing the sun.

I noticed the gulls flying overhead. I followed their motions and saw a small boat a hundred yards up the shoreline. There was a fishing line off the side of the boat. But something didn't feel right. I looked straight at Felix and then straight at the boat. I saw him talk into his radio mike. At the same time I heard Tabby, "The boat is leaving."

The rest of the picnic was filled with food, casseroles, salads, barbecued chicken, and ribs. Stuffed, slightly sun burned, and totally exhausted everyone piled into their cars when the evening mosquitoes came out and headed for home.

My first sight of the ship wasn't impressive. The gravity shuttle approached the construction from below. With no reference points it was impossible to visualize the size of the ship. From the distance, it looked like a child's building toy. The ship was dominated by two features, the front of the ship with its twenty-one-meter parabolic dish and main body, which consisted of a five-meter by twenty-meter cylinder surrounded by six other five by twenty cylinders. Behind the dish and before the cylinders was a partially constructed rectangular box of fifteen meters by ten meters. Aft of the cylinders was another rectangular box but this one was finished. Behind the box was a cluster of spheres and a large maneuvering rocket engine.

As we got closer, I was able to spot the space-suited workers assembling the box by the dish. Inside, I could make out the form of the nuclear reactor and electrical power station for the ship. We circled the ship and came to a cylinder with its end open. With its wings folded against its sides, the shuttle just fit into the fifteen-meter opening. I listened to the huge air lock swing shut and the bay fill with air. Tabby met me when the shuttle door opened. She had been coming up to the ship every day for the last two months.

"Hi, Hon. Ready for the tour of the habitation portion of the ship?"

"Sure but I want to see the control room and look at the

exterior bracing after."

"Well the front half of this cylinder is a shuttle bay with the other half used for storage of oxygen, water, and fuel. The cylinder opposite this one is identical."

"How did you decide on the amount of storage?"

"You know that NASA has never been able to test a complete recycle system and every time the shuttle bay doors open or an air lock we would lose air and water. Well we took the estimated loss that NASA had computed for a five year trip and tripled the numbers. We have the two main storage cylinders plus every section has a balanced storage supply. We should have at least a sixty day supply within the ship even if the recyclers go offline."

"Let's go to the center cylinder?"

The center cylinder had a five-meter tank filled with a bacteria mix for making oxygen and purifying water in the center. Both ends had small gardens laid out around the curved wall. I felt like a hamster walking in a wheel. The front garden was dominated by dwarf fruit trees and a small fountain. We sat on a small bench by the fountain while Tabby told me about the plants. It was the strangest thing looking up and seeing grow lights instead of blue sky. The back garden was all vegetables.

The four remaining cylinders were an exercise/cafeteria unit, secondary crew quarters and equipment storage, a full laboratory and manufacturing shop, and one cylinder for unknown needs. Our living quarters were in half of the aft rectangle. The other half was the bridge of the ship.

The ship was filled with workers. Tabby helped me suit up for the space walk. Three men were assigned to keep me safe while I examined the outside of the ship. I could see the military emblems on their suits so I didn't bother protesting having to be babysat.

"When you finish, I will meet you in our quarters. That's the only place that is currently not under construction. I have all the blueprints and specifications laid out there."

I gave her a kiss, locked down my helmet, and left the

ship with Tom, Dick, and Harry. I got tired of all the *sirs* being uttered at me five minutes into the walk. To retaliate I began actually calling them Tom, Dick, and Harry. The examining of the structural supports, welds, and placement took two hours. The only thing that kept it from being boring was the view of the blue white earth.

Before heading back inside, I took out a half dollar. I tossed it out into space and said, "May this ship be as light as an autumn leaf blown about by a gentle breeze and Nakki be as heavy as this coin pulled to the earth below."

"What was that all about sir?"

"Are you Dick or Harry? Never mind. My grandmother told me stories when I was little about our family history. Some were ship builders and some were sailors. But it was always a custom to speak a protection charm before you sailed. Nakki is an old old name for a malicious and mischievous spirit, a gremlin. You give the spirit, the gremlin, a coin and he follows it down to the bottom of the sea or the planet below while you float away like a leaf."

The matching military triplets shook their heads behind their helmets and followed me to the airlock.

When I got back to the quarters, I found all of the blueprints and spec sheets in our quarters. But I also found Tabby completely naked except for a portion of the blueprints, which she had somehow traced onto her body. I found the gravity control knob for the room and adjusted it for just enough force so everything would eventually make it back to the floor. I did have an interesting time making corrections to the blueprints.

The lab work was slowing down and the construction of the spacecraft was speeding up. Tabby was the engineer so she was busy every day. I took to walking through the woods for hours at a time. I listened to the sounds and felt the breathing of the forest. For some reason my grandmother's stories came back to me stronger than before. I could understand the mythical Finnish hero, Vainamoinen, the singer and knower eternal, the man of quiet waters. The woods, air, water, animals all seemed to form a music of sound. It was as if you could just copy the notes you could become what you heard. I found myself at those times playing with the puukko in my hands, my Great Grandfather Ilmari's steel puukko. Great grandfather was named after the smith Ilmarinen who hammered out the lid of the heavens and the great Sampo. Ilmarinen and Vainamoinen were the best of friends, a poet and an engineer...

"There you are. It is getting dark. Aren't you hungry?"

"Tabby. Do you think it is strange that I am sitting in the woods?"

"No. If I didn't have to work on the spacecraft, I would be sitting here with you."

"Did you ever hear about Vainamoinen and Ilmarinen?"

"No."

"In Finnish mythology they were two friends and heroes. Vainamoinen was a poet who knew too much and Ilmarinen was a builder of the impossible. You know I named the gravity device after Vainamoinen's kantele. I sometimes feel like I know too much."

She tickled me in the side. "You are not Vainamoinen. You are not smart enough." We walked back to the cabin in the falling dusk. I knew there was something more that I had to learn. I seemed to understand science but I now needed to know about the life around me.

***

Santa opened the meeting. "What have you found out about Karpinen?"

Snow White answered, "We have been following him as well as we can with his government guards all around him. We have found no pattern to his movements. We thought about blowing up the spaceship he is building but there is a danger of being discovered by the security measures and it might look like an accident, after all it is the first of its kind.

The same seems to be true with all of his movements. He is too private of a man to be in public regularly."

Hamlet interrupted, "Could we grab someone he loves and pull him away from his protection?"

"Other than his wife we have no idea who would work and she is as well protected as he is."

Santa broke in, "There is always a way. We just have to look harder."

Romeo coughed and everyone turned to look. "I've got an idea..."

***

Tabby needed to talk with Ole face to face and go over plans. We decided to go to LA and the Skunk Works. After telling Felix about the plans, I got invitations for Edwards Air Force Base, JPL, and Dryden Flight Center.

Move-over was shoulder dropping my feet when Felix came back with the list of places that I was *supposed* to visit. During the day, Move-over usually doesn't like to be held but today he molded into my arms when I picked him up. I was upset with the government trying to organize my time so I was a little sharp with Felix.

"We are going to have to have someone feed and water Move-over while we are gone, a bowl of water and scoop of food here and the same at the cabin." Move-over looked at Felix and growled.

"I will take care of it."

"Are you coming or are you staying here."

"Zimmerman has put me on permanent duty as your personal bodyguard."

That was something I had not expected. "Do you want me to talk to him? Tabby's mother Martha was telling me that you were dating Erma's granddaughter Gail."

"How did you know?"

"You're in a small town. Everyone knows everything about everyone."

"Ya. Don't talk to Zimmerman. Ya. He's not the best when it comes to anyone questioning his authority."

"Well you do need a dose of LA to get rid of the Midwest rural slang you picked up."

The trip was different. Manning at JPL had a number of Caltech students for a last minute seminar that I was suppose to speak at. Instead of talking, I brought them to a computer lab and we got to work playing around with equations. Holcum wanted to show off some of the new military equipment at Edwards and Scott and Dr. Jorge were at Dreyden. I wanted to be with Tabby and Ole going over the spaceship plans but I knew I had to put in my time with the others before I could break free.

To pass the time I tried to blend in with all of the people around me the same way I did in the forest. At first, they would try to get me involved with their conversations but my non-committal grunts and ah-ha's slowly stopped them and they soon got to arguing among themselves. It was much harder than understanding the flow in the forest but I eventually seemed to get the feel of the interactions between the people. I got a surprise at Dreyden with Dr. Jorge. He was sitting back and watching the interactions himself. Soon we were sitting together watching the others.

"Why are you watching?"

"What better way to learn about the people around you?"

"Okay, Daniel. Can you tell me the pecking order of the people here?"

"Since you are not participating, I would like to wait before placing you. But Scott is the top dog here. Although, Holcum has a good size following and that man over there has some as well.

"Scott is pretty much ignoring the action and leaving his followers to handle the discussion. Holcum is basically lost. Holcum's aids are trying to insulate him from direct conversation while still trying to affect the superior calm of the military.

"That other man is a different matter. He is challenging Scott for leadership and his people know it. They are trying hard to score points.

"There are about a dozen others who are here either because they need to be or were ordered to be here. They are trying so hard not to be involved that they stand out."

"Interesting observations Daniel. Who is the strongest here?"

I looked him straight in the eye. "I am." I held him with my eyes for a five count and turned back to watching the others.

"So you are Daniel."

"Using my first name is not going to win you any points."

"I know but it is a weakness. I have to try. We are after all people and every social group of animals has a hierarchy. If I can get you to accept my use of your first name, I will be higher on the hierarchy."

"How would you place me?"

"You have natural control over situations but you don't want to be a leader. You are too strong to be a follower. You are a long wolf, an El Lobo. Others can follow where you lead but you are not really a member of the pack. You belong with the pack but are not part of it.

"I've done some reading up on your ethnic heritage and I read a report about your visit to the spaceship. Do you really think that a modern crew can be controlled by a shaman using a simple charm? In the Baltic the Finns are still known as wind wizards but here there is no ethnic history to support using superstition to control people who are not under your immediate command."

Jorge left it there waiting for me to respond. I wasn't going to tell him I did the charm in memory of my grandmother so I just looked at him. After a bit he swallowed hard and turned back to the gathering. I got up.

"Interesting. Good bye Dr. Jorge. I will be leaving now."

Oggie gave us a kitten before we left for our spaceship.

Move-over couldn't decide if he liked the little thing. And he definitely put the kitten in its place when it tried to nurse on him. We had trouble finding a name for the kitten until he fell down the stairs. Tumble and Move-over were going to be the first animals to travel to the outer planets.

Chapter 21
Test Flight

Romeo's plan would take time but Santa thought it was brilliant. It would give the Cell the exact event that they wanted. The *'propaganda of the deed'* would be remembered for centuries. Nothing would go wrong. Hamlet had begged for permission to be the artist for the deed. He knew he would not survive but he also knew his name would be recorded in the history books. Freud, the psychologist for the Cell, started the weeks of hypnotic controls that would be used to protect the Cell if Hamlet was caught still alive. Even the old spy novel trick of hollowing out a tooth for a cyanide pill was done.

Santa was happy. There was so much to do. There was so much passion in the artistic details of the deed. Every member of the Cell felt the excitement. Planning the death of another person was the second most powerful force uniting the Cell. The first was taking part in the killing. For those few people who have the psychological twist that permits murder, there is no greater joy than the killing after a successful hunt.

Hamlet had a wife and children at home but the hard-eyed angular beauty, Snow White screwed him and used him every chance she had until he was exhausted. The sex pushed his already overloaded psyche to the point that all that mattered was killing Daniel Karpinen.

***

The loading of the shuttle was a mess. The last few items of belongings took up most of the spare room in back. The two cats had to be caught a half a dozen times. Whenever the shuttle door was opened, one or the other cat would make a break for it. My greatest surprise during the loading was that Felix would be coming with us. The door was finally shut and we took off with our stocked and ready space shuttle.

The cats decided that this was the best time to play *pounce-your-it*. We were able to keep them off the pilot but both Tabby and I got scratched and Felix was bitten by the kitten. There was no pressing need for speed so the trip to where the spaceship was orbiting took six hours. The cats finally settled down an hour into the trip. The kitten decided to fall asleep draped over my shoulder. Move-over went belly up on Tabby's lap. Tabby was scratching Move-over in his armpits; his rumbling purr was the loudest sound on the shuttle.

Finally through the porthole, I caught my first sight of the completed ship. The outside surface was covered with a yellow Teflon-polymer film. The film was a blend of resins and carbon fibers resulting in a finished coat that was stronger than tungsten steel and able to shed most micro meteorites. The call letters YS2 were printed in black on the large spherical fuel tanks for the maneuvering rockets.

We entered the cylindrical docking bay and opened the doors. The two cats took off with the slinking motion of feline exploration. The first thing Tabby did when we got on board was to announce on the intercom that the christening of the ship would occur in one hour.

I hadn't been active with the final preparations on board for the test run. I knew we were going to be stopping by each of the outer planets in turn and deploying a number of satellites and probes at each planet. NASA had conducted a contest in the schools for projects on each of the planets. Along with the scientific research, there would be real time

Internet feedback to the schools on their projects.

"What is the final count on scientists and technicians that we will be taking?"

"Twenty-one. Schmitt, Manning, and Jorge all insisted on coming. We got a fully trained five man NASA shuttle crew, six of the most skilled members of the construction crew, and four of Holcum's military boys ... Let's see ... that makes eighteen and with the three of us twenty-one. Yup that's the crew."

"On our next trip we will get rid of most if not all of the others."

"Oh really? Just what do you have in mind that we need that much privacy?"

"I was planning on inspecting the blue prints again." Tabby's grin was worth the verbal word play.

The ship's christening was broadcast worldwide. Only four of us went out of the ship, Tabby, two of the NASA crew, and me. The NASA crew videotaped the event. Tabby broke a bottle of water on the side of the ship and pulled the tape off the name.

She had worked on the speech for the last two days after learning that everyone had decided she would be the one doing the christening. After a few false starts, "The Wright brothers took man from walking on the ground to flight within the atmosphere of the earth. In the nineteen-sixties, Russia and NASA took man from our planet into flight within our solar system. This ship will take man and woman from our solar system into flight to the stars beyond. I christen you *Raptor*."

I switched my mike to private conversation. "Short but sweet." I was surprised when I heard tears. "It was fine."

"I couldn't think of anything else to say."

"It was enough. You will see." It was enough. We got selected network TV sent up to us from earth. The public and media fell over each other repeating the short phrase sensing Tabby's emotion in those few words.

We got on board and started to Mars. We were

purposefully taking the planets in order from the sun and not traveling the most economical path. Part of this test flight was to show the versatility of the kantele space/star drive. The main gravity dish started up with Holst's *Planets* playing to fuzzy the electromagnetic waves. I had insisted that we use real music for scrambling the waves with the music being audible in at least the ship's bridge. Most of the artificial gravity spheres in the walls were turned off as the force of gravity from the main dish started to orientate us to down being where the dish was. A tug-of-war between the main kantele dish and the smaller gravity spheres in the 'now' ceiling of the bridge started. Sometimes we felt lighter and at other times heavier. A few of the crew's stomachs couldn't handle the changes but we were prepared with upchuck bags. Slowly, the forces balanced until it was just bearably more than normal g-forces in the living quarters.

It took nine months to deliver all the satellites and probes. The *Raptor* was fast and we didn't stop long at each planet. The gravity gradient produced by the larger dish in the *Raptor* was nearer the needed part of the gravity curve, cutting the velocity required to obtain a tear in the universe's fabric to less than half of the original 200,000,000 meters per second. And by balancing the smaller gravity kanteles in the walls with the main kantele drive, it was possible to accelerate at over 4 g's while only experiencing 1.5 g's in the living quarters.

I did not take a leading role during this trip. I let the NASA pilots make all the decisions with the scientists. I watched and learned. I learned about my new ship and how it runs but mostly I learned about people. People were something I had little experience with. But with twenty-one of us in the small confined space of the *Raptor*, I had the perfect way to learn about them.

Everyone else on board was kept busy. During the stops orbiting the planets, the crews were busy tweaking the ship's design and running experiments. Schmitt became a media figure as he handled most of the scientific briefings that we broadcast to the world. Tabby was in engineering heaven. Oh yes, Tumble became a teenage cat. Move-over resented the changing gravity. Move-over rarely went to the cylinders nearest the main kantele dish with the strongest gravity. But Tumble loved the different forces. With the higher gravity near the drive dish, Tumble could jump across a cylinder with acrobatic displays that looked impossible. Both cats spent most of their rest time in our quarters, the farthest from the drive kantele.

It is hard to describe the outer planets. The colors and views are nowhere as vivid as those produced by the movie studios. But occasionally the real universe can surprise you. In close orbit to Jupiter, it was possible to see the swirling storms and huge atmospheric displays. Some of the dancing colors were reminiscent of the borealis of earth and others seemed to be electrical and plasma bursts of energy. The rings of Saturn were generally blah. There was no color to them except for one brief instant when we passed out of orbit and the nearby light reflected off them in weak rainbow colors.

I should have noticed more about the rest of the planets but it was during the flight to Uranus that I noticed something odd about the ship's flight. The NASA pilots handled the seconds of multidimensional flight with ease and a minimum of midcourse corrections. But I was watching both the pilots and the computer readouts. There was something not planned in the midcourse corrections before dimensional flight. I took to sitting with a laptop by the fountain playing with the tracking information from the flight paths.

We were at Neptune before I got my first hint at what was causing the midcourse corrections. It was simple when the answer came to me. Since man can not make anything uniform, we expected midcourse corrections but the ones I saw were not random and they were larger than the computer projections indicated. We were using gravity as a source in making a dimple in our four dimensional space.

The dimples or creases were easier to make when there were helping gravitational forces and harder to make when there were not. The gravitational power of the large gas planets made the dimpling easier near them and if there was an overlapping of gravitational forces from two or more planets even if they were distant, the crease would have a tendency to migrate with their lines of force.

I talked my findings over with Tabby and we made corrections to the computer guidance programs. The corrections the pilot made in the flight to Pluto and earth were less but they were still there. It is just impossible to have a computer calculate the interactions of multiple gravitational bodies without real time feedback. The three body gravitational problem is one of the classic impossibilities of physics, which is probably why no one thought about the near gravity problem with the kantele drive in the first place.

Tabby came up with the idea of using a force feedback joystick for pilot control with the feedback coming from the course deviation from the planned trajectory. She felt the midcourse corrections would be easier using the joystick. We decided to make the joystick change when we got home to earth.

On a whim, I talked to the two NASA pilots about the control changes. They both acted professional about the information but I was able to see hand and foot movements from one pilot and a deepening of breathing by the other. It was easy to tell that they needed more feedback connection with the controls. And I think they were happy knowing that skill was required to find the best route between two planets. I made a mental note to talk with Tabby about placing some of the control feedback into a foot pedal.

On the last night on board before taking the shuttle down to earth, I closed our cabin door. And adjusted the gravity spheres so there was just enough force in the room to keep us from bouncing off the walls but still low enough that we would sometime drift in the air. It was a glorious end to a trip so full of events I needed the videotapes the crew made to remember details.

NASA and Riley had a huge press event scheduled. Instead of heading for the farm, the landing shuttle transported us to Duluth. We left the cats on board until we could bring them back to our cabin. We landed at the Air Guard Base and convoyed down to the Bay Front Park. Under the tent was a raised dais with a long table. Schmitt, Manning, and the NASA shuttle crew were in the middle. On the left were the four construction crew members. And on the right were Tabby, Jorge, and me. The military men were not to be found and Felix joined the security men on the perimeter of the dais.

Schmitt handled most of the questions and introductions. It was ten minutes into the reporters questioning before Schmitt asked Tabby to answer a question. A reporter had asked why we had cylinders as the main body of the ship and why were they placed sideways and not length wise with the kantele dish.

"We wanted to make as many components of the ship as we could on earth. It is just simpler and cheaper to bring up completed sections and assemble them in space. The best shaped pieces that could be transported into space are rectangular or circular cylinders. The circular ones are stronger. We sent out specification sheets to manufacturers and the five-meter by twenty-meter cylinders from a Winnipeg pipe manufacturer matched what we wanted.

"We didn't want to cut large bay doors into the sides of the cylinders so we put access doors in the ends. The cylinders had to be mounted lengthwise so we could use the doors."

"Mrs. Karpinen, why was the ship painted yellow?"

"We decided we needed a coating..."

My mind drifted from the talk. This was my first chance to watch so many people at one time in nine months.

***

Santa watched everything unfold according to plans. Hamlet was in position. The stage was set. All they needed was the right timing.

***

The reporters in the front rows fidgeted, each struggling to get their questions answered. Some were science reporters and they seemed confident that they would be heard. The national network reporters were commenting from the back waiting for the small one-to-one news segments after the panel discussion ended. The most fun to watch were the locals. They struggled to keep from jumping up or were intimidated by the network people. Behind and to the sides of the news people were the local politicians and a few others with enough pull or money to make it close. And in the back were the masses. The unruly deliciously varied masses. Small children were fighting at the feet of their parents bored with all the talking. I soon spotted the FBI, state police, and Secret Service men watching the crowds. The Secret Service men were here because of the senators and cabinet members sitting to the side and the state police were for the governor. The security men were more interesting than the politicians to watch. They were at least paying attention to what was happening.

***

Romeo was ecstatic. Hamlet passed the security personnel with ease. Romeo was the only other member of the Cell to be near the park. Santa and the others were watching live on CNN. Romeo had to watch everything happen in person. It was his plan. The rest of the world will remember Hamlet as the killer but all in the Cell would know that the real anarchist was Romeo. He smiled and watched.

***

All the riotest variety of people, each different, each with their own set of unique actions; I was awash with sensory overload. It was the first time in my memory that I was happy in a crowd.

A little thing tugged at my mind. Too many people too much action. What was that? Schmitt was saying something about a presentation to me. The Brule Sioux from South Dakota was going to give me a flute. What was that tugging for my attention? It was over near the politicians. No it was next to the politicians. It was a man looking not at the dais or boredly watching the rest of the crowd. There was hunger with his watching. I followed his gaze. He was watching a cameraman.

I turned to Felix and stared at him. I couldn't see his eyes with the dark glasses he had on but I saw him tense. I turned and looked at the watching man. Felix talked into a small mike attached to his lapel. Secret Service moved closer to the man. I knew I could depend on Felix.

The Sioux medicine man walked up to the dais holding a beautiful wooden flute with a red woodpecker head panted on it. I got up and walked around the end of the table watching both the Sioux and the cameraman. The cameraman moved closer as well positioning himself to film the exchange of the flute. I reached out my left hand for the flute. The cameraman tensed as if to brace himself and I saw a finger shake as it stretched to pull a small black lever.

The cameraman was down. My puukko was sticking out of his arm. The man scrambled for the camera with his left hand. He tried to bring the heavy camera back up. Tabby's throwing knife went into his throat and he stopped moving.

I had pushed the Sioux medicine man to the ground, turned and looked at the man who was watching. Behind me, I heard a security man say, "There's a gun in the camera." People were screaming and running. I saw the watching man's face drop in surprise. I started to him. A gulp and he turned to leave but was stopped by a Secret Service man. He turned and another grabbed him. He started to struggle and they took him to the ground.

I was standing over the man. I felt Felix by my side. One of the Secret Service men put his arm up to push me back but Felix stopped him. The handcuffed man had the wide-eyed look of a deer caught in car headlights. I never knew why I did it or how I did it but I started to chant. Chants like the ones my grandmother would tell me about when I was little. I started with Finnish. Finnish seemed to give my words strength. But I somehow I switch the words to English. The chant started so soft no one heard it at first.

"...Kunnella, kunnella.
Listen, listen.
Listen to the cadence
Listen to the tone
See my eyes
Katse sininen
See the shades of blue
Look deep and see your soul
Tell me why
Tell me how
Tell me who
Listen to the quiet waters speak
Hear the sound of the quiet waters
See the water's blue
Talk before you drown
Vainamoinen sing
Kantele breathes
Flute whispers
The man of quiet waters sings
The waters of the earth demand an answer
Talk, talk, talk...
Kunnella, kunnella..."

The man was near a catatonic state but he started to talk. "The Cell ... I belong to the Cell ... We change history by deed..." I left.

Felix whispered, "What did you do?"

"I just asked him why?"

"You know what I mean. You hypnotized him into talking. How the hell did you do that?"

"Do you really want to know?"

I saw him hesitate. He shook his head yes.

"When I was little my grandmother told me about singing runos. In Finland if you knew the right chant or runo and sang it correctly, you could make magic. I don't know if I made magic but I think I understood enough of the man's rhythm to put him in a trance." I didn't want to talk anymore. My words seemed to satisfy him for now. I grabbed Tabitha and said, "I want to go home. I feel older than dirt."

Tabby replied, "You're actually five minutes younger."

"What do you mean?"

"We synchronized an atomic clock on board with one on earth before we took off. It was five minutes twenty-seven seconds and some change slower than the earth clock when we got back."

"Okay, I am five minutes twenty-seven seconds and some change younger than dirt. I don't know about you but that still sounds old to me." She hit me.

We were left alone after what had happened. I caught on the news later in the week that a dozen members of an anarchist group call the Cell had been arrested. The TV showed a heavy-set man with a Santa Claus beard being lead away in handcuffs.

Tabby took the shuttle to the *Raptor* and brought down the two cats. Move-over sauntered out of the shuttle with his normal nonchalance but Tumble was scared of the wide-open sky. When we got to our cabin, Move-over would lie just outside the door teasing the trembling Tumble to come out.

"Move-over you are pathetic teasing the kitten that way."

His only reply was a yowl and a twitch of the tail. Tabby and I left the cats to work out their problems, went inside and held each other by the trickling pool.

I had hired Oggie's son, Harold, to deliver supplies to Uncle Ben when we were gone. He had just made a delivery but we still loaded up a canoe and drifted down the river. We knew he was close when we smelled a wood fire, cedar, birch, maple with the fragrance of roasting meat. Ben met us on the riverbank across from his cabin. He had a campfire with a venison roast cooking on a spit. We ate in silence listening to the trickling water and the crackling of the fire. We never said more than three words in a row to each other but it was still the best homecoming we had.

As we packed up to leave, Ben said, "Bring some salt salmon when you get back from space next time. It goes good with venison."

"How do you know we will leave again so soon?"

"I know. Whatever got you started isn't done with you yet."

Tabby hugged him real hard and gave him a big wet kiss. He turned pink.

We were in the canoe. "Hold it. I forgot to give you this." He ran into the woods and came back with something wrapped in an old gunnysack. It was an ash walking stick like the one he gave Tabby except that it was sized for me. "Remember to bring both your sticks with you when you go this time."

On the woodpecker tree there sat an eagle. His eyes tracked our every move as we paddled up stream to the boat landing.

Tumble started to run after Move-over when he walked outside under the sky so we knew it was time to go again. We loaded up the *Raptor*. In the bridge I had the display screen run through a loop of the various constellations in the sky.

"Okay, where should we go?"

Move-over jumped up and swatted at Orion.

"Gotcha. Orion it is." I put on Holst's *Planets* for the kantele fuzzier. And started down the checklist before our actual leaving earth's orbit. *Venus* was just starting to play when I engaged the kantele drive.

"Tabby, I wonder what music God played when he made the universe?"

"Now don't get philosophical on me. Remember this is just a joy ride."

"What do you want to hear next after Holst is finished?"

"Rachmaninov *Piano Concerto number 2 in C minor.*"

"Thinking about a little romance are we?"

"Of course." She had a saucy simile. "Let's put Grieg on after that. I always wanted to be bounced during *Hall of the Mountain King.*"

"You're twisted. Maybe that's why I love you."

I moved the power setting to full and set the automatic collision warnings and the alarm for just before we got to dimensional travel.

"Hello out there. You better watch out! The Terrans are about to crash the party."

I heard a growl. Move-over was growling at Tumble who was crouched down, shifting his hind legs. Suddenly there was a blur of speed and they were gone into the depths of the ship.

On a near by planet a User infiltrator felt a flutter deep inside. Indigestion? He looked around and saw no one. He still felt a chill. "What in the *damned of the Chameleon* was that?"

Epilog

She was skilled for her age. The fakers of India and the mystics of the Orient didn't come close to her abilities. The mystics only knew hints of the skills that she had already attained. When she concentrated, she could sense every beat of her heart, every change in her body. She had felt her body fighting against itself as the hormones of adolescence surged through her to bring her past puberty to adulthood.

During her daily meditation, she felt the virus enter her body. Using her skills, she sensed the possible problems the disease could inflict upon her. She selected a couple of T cells and the accompanying antibodies to deal with the infection. The T cells in her body were independent entities. They had to be to handle the changing tasks of war with the foreign invader. Non-intelligent entities, although useful, were just too hard to control to fight an infectious virus. To activate the cells, her body released a set of hormones to prepare the T's for the battle ahead.

When she was only a few years younger, she had tried to directly contact her T cells about a problem in her body. But she found out that direct contact changed the cells and made them less flexible in the fight against infections. Her body took what seemed forever to recover from the break down that resulted within her body 65 million internal cycles ago. She still used that method of control for the fight against her own internal problems with the ever-present struggle against cancer and the other degenerative disease's. But she was very careful to keep the contact minimal. A small spiritual awakening and the T cells developed a control group geared to stabilize her metabolism. But with external infections the T cells had to keep their own ability to think creatively. Direct contact with T cells created T cell religions, philosophies, and countries. Those methods frequently stifled growth and flexibility. T cells had to grow and expand to deal with external threats. That was why she had to communicate with them using the intermediaries of the antibodies. Antibodies were simpler creatures, semi-intelligent organic or mechanical things, easy to control and manipulate. They could also communicate with the T cells by their physical presence.

Her selection of T cells was easy to make. She tweaked the curiosity of the primary T cell in such a way as to attract the attention of the virus. She gave the T cell a full compliment of antibodies to help with the job and then to play it safe she introduced the cell to another T who had a natural sensitivity to the virus. Her next step was to activate their defensive structure by introducing a vaccine created by local group of T cells that had been damaged. The destruction of the damaged cells proved to her that her choice of defense was sound. But she was surprised at how easily the newly tested group of cells destroyed the virus.

She was getting older and had started noticing the neighborhood *boys* eons ago. She had been watching the young man who lived in the neighborhood her T cells called the Orion constellation. Maybe it was time to formally introduce herself to him? This last group of T cells showed themselves to be exceptionally adept at survival. They needed only a few more exposures to other internal cancers to get them ready. They should make the trip easily to his body. She would have to make sure her cells used her proper name, Terra. She always hated the nickname the family hung on her of Earth.

When this group of T cells came back from introducing her, she would have to give them a reward. Maybe some time off to regroup and multiply. She had a feeling that those viruses were still around.

The End

Biography

Forsaking life in town, S. A. Gorden lives with his family in semi-seclusion in the northern woods of Minnesota. He graduated from a Midwestern college in the 70's with university degrees in physics, mathematics and computers. He has had jobs ranging from day labor in the logging industry to civilian contract work for the United States Air Force. His previous employment includes a managerial position with the second largest computer manufacturer in the world. He currently works occasionally as an instructor, an independent consultant, and as a full-time stay at home father. But most of his free time is spent in the forest behind his home, cutting firewood and lumber or just enjoying the quiet of the woods.

Gorden has written five novels and his short stories have appeared in various periodicals and anthologies. Email can be sent to gorden_sa@hotmail.com.